Just Take Charlie

KIMBER CROSS

ISBN: 1494411571
ISBN-13: 978-1494411572

For you.

CONTENTS

ACKNOWLEDGMENTS

Thank you OF, MJR, NDS and AG.

And LRB, always LRB.

BRAVO

Christmas Day 1997. A week before my fifteenth birthday and I am riding around in the back of a blue Ford Cortina. The guy who is driving will be dead in less than a month. Of course I don't know that now, but I find out. Actually I'm there when it happens, but a month is practically forever away.

The other people in the car are running late, so late in fact they don't want to talk to me or anyone else. I sit wedged between them as they stare at the back of Jack's head. He hums and taps his fingers on the steering wheel. This annoys the late people. Late people can't be driven around by someone as nonchalant as this, so they use all their willpower to force their son to drive faster. And that is the deal. They push him and push him and in return he falls. It's not as bad as it seems; the drive will only last twenty minutes.

To pass the time I stare at the pile of jellies and blancmanges stacked high in the front passenger seat. The top jelly has a short dark hair resting beneath the surface. I'd bet its Jack's mother's but it could equally belong to the family dog.

Five minutes before we reach our destination, Jack's mother begins to talk. She knows it is safe enough now – no awkward situations can emerge in such a short time. She talks at him, her head bobbing up and down with the pitch of her voice and I'm fixed on her snitchy old mouth making a series of little Os, like an eager goldfish.

Whenever she does this, no matter how hard I try, I cannot stop myself thinking about her giving head. Not to me. To her husband, I guess.

She yaps away, about Boxing Day and Jack's grandparents coming down from wherever they live in the north where it's dark and poor and no-one owns a car. Jack nods along, maybe to her, maybe to the music.

What's that breed of dog called, the one that always slobbers? Trails of white spit just hanging off its face. Why doesn't it do anything about it? Why is the spit so white? Looks like jizz. If one dog spaffed on another of those dogs, would anyone even notice? Other people must think about this kind of thing. I'm not the only one.

Someone says my name but I pretend to ignore it and instead I plaster on a smile, and lean over Jack's dad to look out the window. We roll past rows of suburban houses, all with the exact same square of lawn, the same big tree at the front. Occasionally there's a plastic Santa or a dog that someone's forgotten to take in for the night, running in circles on its leash. These differences are the only indication we're moving at all.

Jack's mother is about to flip. Her voice is raspy and wet, like her tongue is drowning in her mouth. I stare at my scuffed knees, trying to think of something else, but when I look back up her whole face is orange-pink like the salmon you see in the fishmonger's window.

I can't understand the words bubbling out of her mouth and by this point I imagine her gagging on fluids, flushed and sweating, somehow still fighting. The dog breed I'm thinking of is called the *Saint Bernard.* I knew I knew it.

We reach the stop off. Jack focuses on steering the car hard into the curb and I wonder what he'd think if he knew what was going through my head.

His mother, halted for a moment by the bump of the Ford mounting the pavement, is silenced and all the men in the car breathe a sigh of relief.

As the engine cuts out she leans over and pecks me on the cheek. Instinctively I sniff, searching for some trace of semen. Nothing. Just chemicals masking that old lady smell, like her insides have rotten away and now she's trying to hide it. Maybe that's how they all smell, I don't get to be this close to many grown women.

'Merry Christmas Charlie,' she says.

'Merry Christmas,' I echo.

Jack's father doesn't say anything but then maybe that's because I caught him checking out my arse last week.

Then they're gone, taking their hairy food with them.

I climb over to the front seat. The cracked imitation leather feels cold against my thighs. Jack turns up the music and we start to drive.

It's Christmas Day and a week before my fifteenth birthday. The problem with having your birthday on New Year's Day is as the clock strikes twelve no-one is sober enough to celebrate with you.

Call me old fashioned, but if they're not sober enough to stand, they are not sober enough to screw and that means the start of my birthday is never fun at all. I'm not so desperate to take the ones that have passed out, not yet anyway. We've all seen that one film *KIDS.*

All I can do is say a prayer that one of the drunk girls at this Christmas party will be good enough to relieve me of my Virginity and hope I score tonight instead. I've attached some mistletoe to my belt buckle in anticipation.

We're heading for a party just two roads away. The big detached house, with a gravel drive and bright green lawn, might be a clone of all the others in this road, this entire town, but behind the door it's a world away from cheese and charades.

The guy who is holding this party is a real arsehole, but his little sister is hot. She's not shy either, or so I've heard. That's why I'm here.

And Jack? Jack goes anywhere.

We trample across the bright green lawn and Jack complains that his trainers are getting wet despite the fact it hasn't rained in days.

For some reason, maybe because he had a couple of joints before he left the house, or maybe because he never was the smartest in his year, it takes him a good thirty seconds before he notices the clicking of the sprinklers spraying water in every direction to keep the lawn plush.

There's no bell, just a giant brass knocker in the shape of some monster beast and I start pounding on the ugly head to be heard over the music while Jack wipes his trainers against one of those little trees shaped like a ball.

The arsehole with the hot sister opens the door of his huge house and poses with one hand stuck to his crotch. I've not seen him this close before. He's on the sixth form wrestling team and it shows. His arms are like hams which make the hand clasped around his package look like a small pink pincer.

I can't explain it, but every bone in my body wants to collide with his. I can feel the pressure burning in my arms, the sour taste in my mouth every time I look at him and find myself thinking that I don't care how big he is, I would love to just get one good hit in, one smack to the jaw before he pummeled me into the ground.

I can tell he doesn't like the look of me either and I try and hide my disgust by keeping my eyes low and I fiddle with the hem of my dress while he asks Jack how we know each other.

I don't hear what Jack says, but it must be good because our host's hand has gone straight from his crotch to shake mine. I don't want to do it, but I know I have to. I console myself with the fact that by the end of the evening I plan for this hand to be inside his little sister.

We walk past him into the house, but I can still feel his eyes on me. There's something about this guy that doesn't fit, yeah he's all dumb muscle and he looks at me like most of the sports kids do: with a repulsion so obvious you'd think they were chewing tin foil, but after that he keeps on looking.

I back down, this is his house and I guess he's got his entire team of wrestlers here tonight anyway.

Besides, so what if he could take me in a fight? He's got nothing on me apart from a few pounds of muscle. The guy must be nearly eighteen and hasn't kissed a girl, let alone fucked one. I draw my nasty conclusions, file them away in my little brain and move on. Every picture can get a little bit bigger and I'm sure his is just about to spill right off the page.

Over the stereo Billy Corgan makes us fall in love with a year before any of us were born and the air tastes thick with sweat. Already I am caught up halfway on the makeshift dance floor in the middle of the living room and the music is so loud that it feels like the bass line of the song is being played directly onto my ribcage.

Kids snake around the edges of the room, moving back and forth in ant lines leading to crates of beer, piles of CDs, a bong someone has knocked over and picked up again, and a porn magazine with all the pages ripped.

This is just the first room and as I stand among the dancers, I can picture how massive the whole house is, how it must be three times the size of mine, and tonight it could be brought to the ground by a hundred fucked teenagers.

Between the drawn curtains you can catch glimpses of the floodlights that hit the house from every angle, making it seem like it's still daylight outside. Of course anything could be going on, we could be surrounded by squad cars, or it could be a case of divine intervention – God Himself appearing on the lawn to change the fate of some stranded kid and no one in here would see. And for this one moment I want to be anywhere but here.

But I'm here, inside this rich stranger's house with flood lights shining through the curtain cracks and pulsing next to me are all the people I know, all the freaks and fuck-ups I spend my days with. Everyone here has problems and I zone in and out trying to change frequency to not get caught up in them.

My peers you see, they can't help it, they have to draw you in and they're all here, each with their own story. The girl that's in love with her Papa, the boy who said he had a brain tumour and tuberculosis and AIDS five years ago and is *still* alive, the scholarship student in her third term of college and first term of pregnancy.

They all need their fifteen minutes, but its fifteen minutes from you every time you walk by. I just don't have time for another sex abuse sob story.

Get over it or let it kill you. That's my motto.

I fight my way toward a bucket of former ice and cheap European beer in squat brown bottles. I pull a beer, crunch the top with my molars and try to mask the wince of pain. The beer is bitter and fizzy, leaving my tongue feeling dryer than before I drank. I down the liquid in four glugs and drop the bottle on the floor where the sweat on the bottle leaves a little mark on the carpet. A small victory against the arsehole or his parent's cleaner.

Keep moving, nods to the kid whose mother's Polaroid had visited every greasy hand in my school year, captured in a wipe clean format throughout time. The girl with the bleach drinking problem, the boy who saw a fatal car crash at five. No conversations, no contact.

They all turn out here on Christmas Day because they hate their families or their families hate them.

I've heard there's a girl with two anuses and although I've not seen them, I've heard she puts them to good use. Perhaps she should issue out sex advice to the two per cent of girls that are pregnant at my school.

And everyone here has problems and everyone here has no one.

Just like me.

But what really scares me, deep down is how they make me feel. All these kids fighting for attention, I just want to stop them in their tracks, dead. Take away their issues and their counselling session. Cut off *The Samaritans*, cut off *Child Line*. Stop them and give them something real to worry about.

I want to be that thing.

I'm cruising round for the hot little sister and she's nowhere to be seen.

Jack has miraculously pinned himself to the multiple anus girl, when I walk past she is tugging at her tight black fringe, nodding frantically. I can hear him trying to convince her to go on a late night Japanese betting show – where he's sure she could get paid to let lots of people bet on her bowel movements.

He's not going to get anywhere.

Everybody knows only one of the anuses is functional.

I don't know why she lets him talk to her like that. I guess she just likes to talk about her problem. Or maybe she is just pleased to be talking to a man who isn't asking to screw her bonus hole. The girl is named Lucinda which was shortened to Cindy. Since the anuses issue came out she's known as Butt-Fuck Barbie. Some people have all the fun.

Me, I get to keep my own name, the same name as Papa before me. My past is like everyone else's and I'm not here to spill my history with my guts after one bottle of warm beer.

Just take Charlie. Charlie like my Papa, like Charlie Brown, Charles Manson, Charlotte Bronte, or a line of Charlie.

Then she appears, the hot little number. In the middle of my dazed dream she has found me. I was all up for stalking her, taking my time and working my charms and here she is in front of me all smiles and vodka punch, wincing as she unhooks her pants from where they've gotten stuck.

We're wearing almost the same outfit; a black dress with dungaree buckles, the difference being my padded bra and the contents of my jockeys. And she seems to be wearing a lot of tinsel and furry slippers.

'Jack isn't it?' she asks knowing it's not. For a moment – just a moment I'm tempted to say yes, then tomorrow when she confesses all to her parents returning home from some wife swapping party she can tell them it was Jack that ripped her hymen open on their three hundred pound sheets from Harrods.

'We've been at the same school for three years,' I tell her, 'it's Charlie.'

She pulls a face, 'You're sweet,' she tries, then she trails off or maybe I just stop listening. I tell myself I should be a little nicer. I've still got to get her up a few flights of stairs after all.

'So where are your parents tonight?' I ask, pleased with my feigned interest.

'Who knows, probably at some wife swapping party.'

Catching the stunned expression I'm sporting, she thinks I'm shocked at her comment. I force a smile, trying to hide the jolt of coincidence. One cheap joke and I think she can read my mind. I notice my arms are shaking, she sees it too. Maybe it's the big V, waiting to escape.

'It's ok, Michael's here - and his friends, he'll make sure everyone is safe.'

'Michael?'

'Yeah, my brother. I thought you knew him, didn't he invite you?'

'Does it matter?'

Twenty minutes later and her parent's sheets aren't as expensive as I'd have imagined. She looks nervous, but she doesn't know half the deal yet. In the next room I can hear someone playing some eighties reject metal track. I pause a second, craning my head away from the girl, straining to listen *there's no escape, now* and underneath the music a couple humping. The lyric seems so fitting, like the soundtrack to some slasher film that I want to hum it over and over to her until she gets the point.

She will never get the point.

She kisses like a little girl pretending to be a woman and she tastes like one too – bubblegum and vodka. I pull down my dress and tuck the content of my jockeys away the best I can as she reaches for the padded cup of the itchy bra covering my flat, flat chest and I think *(did I?) did I shave?* Sometimes I leave the stubble there, not often, just occasionally. I run my fingers over my own chest, an action that can only be interpreted as vain, but I need to do it. The skin feels smooth enough. I can't wait to surprise her with my dick.

Unhooking her dress I tell her she can't tell anyone if she wants us to do this, she can't even think of it, and as it comes off over her head she replies a little to my surprise, that she won't tell anyone – not even her brother Michael.

Mentioning the brother at a time like this was a little unexpected, but then I've found it's the notches in people that make them memorable, all the faults that don't speak - the ones they don't know about in themselves.

Her thumbs hook into the sides of her pants and pull them down in one swift movement. She's done this before, that or she's copied her moves from *MTV*. There's no bra and she doesn't need one.

Barely fourteen, her body is small and not completely developed. Her breasts are still perfectly upturned, gravity hasn't found her yet. Her stomach is a small rectangle of flat muscle and I figure she must play sport. Maybe the volleyball team - but her breasts are too small, Lacrosse? No, she's not *that* rich. Then my mind falls back to summer; Jack and I in the baking sun watching the bitches from the private school playing Tennis.

I slot this girl amongst them in their tight, white kits. Think of another girl brushing her hair aside, an accidental stroke of bare thigh, firm and almost tan.

And here she is, legs spread wide, a small pink glow between them, feet disappearing into furry bear slippers. Both of us glistening with sweat. Her skin tastes salty and raw.

The heat is unbearable. It's as if the air has been sucked out of the room. I wish I knew what I was doing. I try to work out what this girl's name might be. Tracey, Louise, Vikki, Janea. I imagine her doing her homework; try to focus on the name on the front.

A drop of sweat falls from my forehead and lands on her abdomen and instantly it's all I can focus on. I watch it trickle lower until it is lost amongst the thick matt of her pubic hair. She hasn't learnt to shave yet and the waxy curls spread to the edge of her thighs and creep up her stomach. I let my gaze wander higher, and I'm trembling now as I run my hands over her body. Gliding upward my fingers wrap perfectly round her stiff little neck.

Finally I feel like I am in the moment, like the music is guiding me, and then I look at her; I can just about make out the shape of her chin her where her head is flung back and I'm thinking of that seventies video Mr. Thompson showed us of a woman giving birth in sex ed.

Mr. Thompson served in the Falklands and even he looked shocked. The vagina is a birth canal. That's just not sexy. I do not want to put my thing in it. It's over as quickly as it started. My Virginity shrivels up and crawls back inside me.

Porn lied to me. This isn't fun at all.

There's nothing left but to leave a lasting impression. I bite the insides of her thighs leaving big red and purple rounds until she's asking me to stop – it's too hard. So I fumble around in my new designer bag, a bag I'm sure this girl's parents would approve of. I'm searching for something to put inside her, but all I have are my essentials. A collection of crap that reveals my sex more than my cheap hair extensions or over-developed thighs.

I finger each item quickly with my spare hand, identifying each by touch. My curve jawed pliers - too sharp, a pair of plastic sunglasses broken in two – too slippy, and the only item that seems half suitable: my trusty socket wrench. Perfect for fixing up the bike or warding off potential thugs. Manufactured from chrome vanadium steel, hardened, tempered and polished for corrosion protection. Tonight, I think it's going to need it.

The metal feels cool to the touch and she flinches slightly when she feels it slide across her damp skin and then inside her future birth canal. She groans and writhes, like Linda Blair's body double and she's pretty loud for someone trying to be discreet.

'I'm not a lesbian you know,' she confides between bursts. I push the wrench higher, the knurled grip grating the skin off the tips of my fingers. 'You want me to be a lesbian don't you?' She can't see what's inside her from here and I wonder what she'd think if she knew of all the dirt and grease worn into the metal.

'I want you to make less noise.' I say. Her nails dig into the soft sheets as her body leads her to a fake climax. I push until I can only hold the last two inches and her spine seems to bend wildly out of shape. She takes it all and I wait until she collapses onto the mattress before I pull the wrench out slowly. I wipe off the gloop on the sheets without looking, while I wait for her to speak.

'I've never done it with a girl before,' she gasps. *You haven't had one now* I think. 'It's just you're so sexy, you know and really pretty.' Was that a joke? I'd ask her but she's turned her head away from me.

I take one last look at her now limp body, eyes closed and cheeks flushed. Either I wore her out or this is my cue to exit. For a moment I hold my hand just above her cunt to feel the heat and wait for the little beads of sweat to do their job. There's brown-red smeared across her thighs and matted into her fluffy slippers but I'm sure it's just period or something.

I've wiped most of the slime off the wrench, but the evidence is still there, mixing with the grease and smelling coppery.

It's only now that I realise with horror that the socket is missing. She can't have sucked it into her vortex. How will I fix my bike now? It's only a shitty little racer I use to get around when Jack isn't about, but it's my only independent transport and it's already in need of a few repairs.

The girl curls over, eyes still glued closed, feigning sex bliss, another pose she's mastered. Who am I to talk? I'm more of a liar than she is – but in my mind I didn't really deceive her, my gender is there for all to see, she just decided not to see it. There's nothing wrong with that, I do it myself.

The parent's bedroom is pretty minimal. The walls consist of a few prints by some guy named Constable who I've never even heard of, some thick curtains a nasty drill job that's all plaster holding a sconce in place. The kind of thing Papa would tut at.

In the top bedside draw I find two folded twenties and a bottle of lubricant. It's amazing what you can discover about people through a little detective work, cash just lying around and a sex aid worth sixty pence, one step away from saliva and petroleum jelly. I guess this is proof adults don't do it that often.

I take one last look at her, before turning around and heaving my Virginity out the door with me.

I wake up at home, on the sofa with Matka leaning over me.

'I thought there was a girl involved. There usually is,' she tells me.

With no poor relations of our own, I spend Boxing Day with Matka. We sit in our old towelling dressing gowns, eating stale babka and she quizzes me about my evening, asking where Jack is and whether I kept my hair tied back.

She never comes out and asks me if I dressed in my own clothes or a girl's but seeing as she must have been the one to put me in my dressing gown I'm guessing she knows. I'm not even sure how she feels about it. With Matka, one cold stare and she'll shrink back into her own head. I just can't help giving those stares sometimes. I guess it comes from Papa.

'Jack's with his family ma, I've told you he's not with a girl.'

One thing I do know, Matka doesn't like it when Jack and I spend too much time together – she thinks it's bad for our health. As if screwing an underage girl with an older wrestler-type brother isn't. When she finds Jack is out with a girl – or gone cruising in the blue Ford, she gets upset that he's neglecting me. I can't win. It's as if she nurtures my emotions for me and allows me to peek at them on special occasions.

What occasions are more special than Christmas and Birthdays?

She asks if I was warm enough and if I took a coat, and what she means is, did I dress outside of my gender? She asks if I met anyone nice, because when boys my age come home late, there's usually a girl involved and my paranoia means I am sure she is trying to ask if I dress like a girl, do I act like one between the sheets? Or for kids my age, in the back of cars or the bushes in a park.

These questions are easy and really, I breeze through the answers. But then comes the hard stuff and as she starts I prepare my poker face that I learnt from *The Antiques Roadshow.*

Matka asks if I remember last night fully, if there were any blank spots or parts that were hazy. This is because sometimes, not that often, I kind of forget stuff. And yeah, okay, it happened last night. I switch to the poker face and when she doesn't eat it up, I shoot her *the look* and she actually flinches so I smile until her shoulders drop. This buys me enough time to get my story straight.

The last thing in focus was leaving the girl, the expensive bedroom, opening the door into the hall and tucking the forty pounds in my stocking tops, which are by now probably laddered to shit. I know the forty pounds is still there but after that I draw a big blank.

'No, everything is just where it should be, Matka. You know I'd tell you if I was having problems again.' Big smile, the Oscar winning portrayal of clean cut boy goes to Charlie Lewandowski.

'How did you get home last night?' she asks and I know this is a trap. Even if she doesn't come downstairs, ever since Papa left she's always stayed awake, waiting for me to come home. God, she probably opened the front door for me.

'I got a lift. With Jack.' I make it a statement and keep up the eye contact 'You were there after all.' I run my hand through my hair, try to act like its short and gelled, not long and knotted.

'Okay Charlie, there was just a little blood on your shoes – I thought maybe you'd got into trouble again.'

But it wasn't trouble I got into.

I've passed the test and her meek voice filters through flashbacks of last night. What can I say? *Don't worry mum, I was just sticking tools up this girl and it got a bit rough?* Besides, everyone goes on about me getting into trouble. They've not seen anything yet.

Trouble is going down alleys with boys from out of town. It's writing your phone number in a toilet stall. It's killing your best friend. That's trouble.

At six o'clock the phone rings and it's Jack. I know it's him because no-one else calls here. Matka answers and by six-fifteen she's handed the phone over to me. When I put my ear to the receiver I can still hear Jack's polite laughter and his 'good to speak to you Mrs. L' like we're all in *Happy Days*.

I ask if his poor relatives were amazed with the central heating, but he cuts me short – he's telling me a girl at the party last night was raped.

'Barbie..?' I guess.

'No, not fucking Barbie – Jesus Charlie,' then I remember last time I saw Barbie she was with Jack.

'Sorry mate, I was just making an educated guess,' I start to mumble.

'Charlie – listen Charlie, it was Kate.'

'Kate? That's just terrible, mate, terrible. Wait – who the fuck is Kate?'

'Kate, Katie! Katie Rowan.'

'Oh,' I say.

'Charlie, Katie is Michael's sister, you know Michael it was his fucking party.'

'Oh,' I say again, as if I care.

I wait for Jack to hang up and listen for the dialing tone of the telephone. After a minute the recorded woman informs me that the other person has hung up and it's time to replace the handset.

I wish there were instructions like that for everything in life. Where is she when it comes to real advice? I bet she never made a tape for *you may be accused of raping an underage girl, but you don't remember if you did it*. I bet she has never even said the word rape.

Before we said goodbye Jack told me the Police would have gone all *Columbo* and collected evidence by now. DNA samples and statements and whatever else they do so well. They would have semen samples, hair samples, skin samples. Did I do it? He asked clear and open. *Did I do it?*

The fact is, I don't know, or more accurately I can't remember and each time I try to go back to that moment of opening the door to leave I keep imagining that textbook with a girl's name suddenly coming into sharp focus.

Her name is Katie Rowan and someone raped her. I tell Jack *No, I didn't* - but I can't bring myself to say the words. Perhaps that'll help me look innocent if it comes to court. What I mean is *No, I don't think so*. But *I don't think so* is something you say when your parents ask if you remembered to take the rubbish out, not when someone asks if you forced a girl to have sex with you.

I just forget things, that's all. The doctor calls them blackouts, but they're more like grey-outs really. This means I am in control of what I am doing at the time, I just can't tell you what it was I did the next day. Like an alcoholic. He thinks I don't want to remember. So when I think back to some crappy thing I did everything fades and slows like watching someone die on *Dallas*.

Sometimes I can shake them off but most of the time everything just greys out and then time jumps and I'm lying in my bed with all my clothes on and sick slowly drying in my hair.

That's how I found myself this morning. Forty pounds richer and accused of rape. That isn't true, no one has accused me of anything yet, not even of having a penis. But she knew I was a boy, I should have noticed at the time. What was the first thing she said to me? *Jack isn't it?*

So she knew, right from the beginning. My face flushes at the thought of being so see-through, especially to another kid my age.

Then why did she bother going through all that talk about going with another girl? Maybe that's what she's into, or she just thought I wanted to hear it.

Maybe she's got a Virginity of her own to get rid of. It looks like she's sorted that out now for sure.
She seemed so in control. Like that whole scene was what she did every night. She had every other move rehearsed, straight out of *Cosmo*. *Ten ways to lure a lover.*

She'd got that sleazy school girl routine down perfectly. A grind of the hips, a flick of the hair, a pout of the lips and back to the beginning. Now I'm hoping the wounded victim is just another part she can play.

Or did I do it? After the grey edges faded into the middle did I change my mind, go back and fuck Katie? Am I a Virgin?

I try to feel if my body seems different, lighter, am I without the big V? If only boys had hymens, then I could check. If I did go back into that room and fuck Katie Rowan did she protest?

God, was she even conscious?

'Men are such bastards,' Matka once said.

'Then believe me I am the worst one,' Papa replied.

Charlie Senior left one winter night long ago, I don't remember when exactly, neither does she. It was as if he seeped through the thin plaster walls bit by bit into the next flat until one night he wasn't there anymore. His shadow was gone from the hallway and then his dark smell, home from some strange place I couldn't know about.

The arguments ceased because he ceased. I stopped hearing his voice outside my bedroom door last of all. For a long time after Papa left I missed the instability he had brought, I wanted to harness it and make it my own. He was never mentioned except when I was bad Matka would occasionally say *don't do that Charlie, you know Papa doesn't like it.*

When I was small, I loved who Papa was. He was Charlie the Pirate, Charlie the Thief, the disappearing act – as sleek as night itself. I didn't see him as an oppressor of Matka, dictator of three, the one that made her cry and bleed. Matka says what the eyes and the heart see are two different things. She also says listen to your Papa. And that back in Poland this sort of thing is normal.

He ruled the house, above me, above Matka. When he first left I wondered how long it would be before I would take his place.

Would I be capable of that?

Like my namesake do I have the power to be the worst kind of man? Papa was able to turn any object into an instrument of torture. I don't just mean kitchen knives and heating irons. I mean doorstops and roadmaps, side lamps and candelabras.

Was it that kind of power I held? To make people want to spit at you in the street because you hurt their loved ones?

The kind of power that stopped the grocer and milkman from looking you in the eye, that made your wife plan each sentence before she spoke?

Sometimes I think if that is true I don't want to be any kind of man at all. That's when the dresses started to look good.

Then there are other times, times when I get so completely fuelled by anger I can taste it like acid eating away at my tongue, feel it coiling in my muscles as my arms get ready to hit out at whoever deserves it.

I burned down an allotment shed once, no one found out and only Jack saw, but it didn't take the anger away so it was pointless. As the flames grew out of control I knew the fire didn't need me, so all the anger built up inside my body couldn't get out.

I spent the week after shitting myself every time Papa came home from work, thinking he'd have heard about it or somehow he would smell the smoke imprinted on my skin.

I knew sooner or later he would be needing to release his own anger out on me.

I've decided that once something bad has happened to you, you have to carry it around with you like this burning hot coal. Sometimes you can put it in your pocket and almost forget about it, but it's always there, smoldering away.

When things get really bad the only thing you can do is hurt someone else, let it all flow out onto them instead and for that short time, they have to carry the coal.

The problem is when you're done, you've got to take it back and by that time the person you've hurt has already got a little coal nugget of their own. Most of the time, Papa is so rough with me I reckon he's lugging round an entire mine.

Now, faced with an accusation of rape, I can hear my heartbeat in my cars and feel it pulse in my belly, just like after the fire.

My throat starts knitting together and I swear I won't be able to breathe if it doesn't stop soon. I try to think of what you're told to do when your body betrays you in

19

panic. Am I supposed to drink a glass of water or put my hands above my head or something? What would Matka say to calm her fretful son? The words I hear are *you brought it on yourself.*

I feel like a criminal. I am a criminal, possibly. Perhaps I'll just get the next train out of here, just start heading towards another big city and see where I end up.

I am not designed for crime. My belly is yellow, but not until the morning after. If I could only be a coward in the heat of the moment all my problems would go away.

What if I didn't do anything? I just have to remember what happened after I left Katie, but I know I can't. I never remember - it just doesn't work like that. Once it's gone, it's gone.

I thought about phoning her, the girl - but I'd already checked the phone book while I was talking to Jack, there were so many Rowans and I couldn't remember her address or anything other than the fact she lived in a rich part of town.

So I do the only thing I can and go a little *Columbo* myself.

It's Boxing Day, 1997, seven o'clock in the evening and while the nation eats cold turkey sandwiches I wheel my bike from the hallway onto the concrete outside. Matka seems pleased that I'm going for a healthy bike ride, dressed as a healthy boy, until she catches sight of my back pocket.

'Where are you going that you need a bike and a hammer?' Matka demands.

I don't know what I was planning to do with it – just scare her I guess.

I would never try to kill her – that would be plain crazy. She's not worth that by any means.

Anyway I am still guessing I'm innocent until I prove myself guilty.

'Jack needs to borrow it,' I lie.

'Well make sure you bring it back – you know it belongs to Papa.'

'Like he's ever going to come and get it.' I mumble, but she doesn't hear or doesn't want to.

The brakes on the racer are worn down to nothing and it's hard to change gears without the chain falling loose. My repair kit and the designer handbag holding it are under my bed, waiting to be cleaned.

Despite the fact it's December I am wearing very little and the cold rushes through me, forcing me to peddle faster.

I was hoping the bitter weather would clear my mind, prepare me for whatever awaits me on Katie's carefully cut lawn somewhere on the good side of town, but my head will not allow me a glimpse of the past let alone a reliable interpretation of the future.

I'd been reckless already, phoning every girl I'd ever spoken to, trying to find out about Katie. Most refused to speak to me, rumours were spreading.

But I was sure if I could get a better idea of who she was I might be able to work out what she wanted out of this. It seemed worth the risk, and I was right.

Katie is not the pop princess you might expect and a number of girls were willing to talk to me despite my growing cross-dressing rapist reputation.

Twelve hours ago I didn't know her name, now I had a bitchy schoolgirl report on her activities from what gum she chewed (Juicy Fruit, the very breakfast of champions) to how many boys she'd gone down on last summer break (a moderate seven).

It wasn't too hard, everyone was talking about her and I knew I couldn't ask for her address but everything else was offered up for sale. Still I couldn't work out what would happen when I got to her house.

Maybe Michael and his wrestler friends will be waiting in case I prove to be stupid enough to show up, to ask to be punished for this crime. Or her rich parents awkwardly sitting with the Police, inconvenienced by their soiled sheets and soiled daughter.

I'm an expert on the Rowans now, thanks to the fact Katie's friends all have parents in Neighbourhood Watch.

I know just as well as she does her parents will see this whole incident as a smear on their reputation, another pie in the face for the Rowan family and their wayward daughter.

Katie was born in 1983 into the rich Rowan household. At the same time, according to Encarta, the Conservative party gained a landslide victory in the General Election with Margaret Thatcher winning her second term in office as Prime Minister, a double celebration for the Rowans.

Her older brother Michael was there at her birth and it was Michael, not her dad, who was chosen to cut the cord between Katie and their mother.

Mr. and Mrs. Rowan were not the kind of parents to be worried by miner's strikes or anti-nuclear demonstrations. They were worried about the cars in their drive and labels in their shirts.

The picture starts coming together.

A comfortable suburban lifestyle bored Katie and she looked for excitement wherever it could be found. Unlike Michael, she did not excel in any one subject at school, she was rich and she was popular, she wasn't particularly dumb or smart – she just needed attention.

She learnt to hang out with the alternative kids at school and her image slowly changed from Popular Princess to High School Harlot. She cut her classic blonde locks and replaced them with tufts of coloured hair. She didn't understand the new music she'd found but did understand the boys.

At home she would hang off the friends Michael brought to visit, much to his distaste. To him it seemed like a sick joke, these guys were his friends, his wrestling partners, his idols and she was banging them one after another.

Katie knew it angered her brother and it was this more than anything that drove her to continue working her way through all the boys she could find.

By then she wasn't popular anywhere other than bike sheds and back seats of cars, the only thing she had was a nasty reputation. That's when I stepped in.

I should seriously consider becoming a detective.

My calves are stinging from cycling so hard and my eyes are streaming from the cold. It's almost eight o'clock now and the night sky is not blue, but black.

It's Boxing Day, 1997. Six days before my fifteenth birthday and I'm accused of Rape, capital R.

I try to cycle in and out of the yellow pools of light looking like a rich kid on a bike, with all sixteen ounces of high carbon steel claw hammer burning in my back pocket.

It's ten before I find her. Turning into a road that looks like all the others, I've taken to trying wheelies on my racer just for a bit of excitement. Boredom is the answer to fear.

If the end of the world was three years away people would settle down after the first month of shock. Wait for long enough and everything dulls, even fear.

Like an oversized Gnome she stands in the front garden, the moonlight drawing one side of her face sharply into focus. She looks even younger than before.

It's as if in twenty four hours she has shrunk to half her size.

Was I responsible for this malformation?

She isn't moving, perhaps she is bait to catch me? Michael and her parents hidden in the shrubs, the Police behind the fir trees. No, unreasonable; the Rowans wouldn't sacrifice Katie like that. I could be dangerous.

She doesn't even flinch as I approach her, which impresses me. I keep waiting for those huge flood lights to kick in, neighbours to drag me off and hold me in their basement until the Police arrive.

At some point I've taken the hammer from my pocket and now I'm holding it, the rubber grip feeling sweaty in my hand. I'm standing in front of her looking into her bruised face. She is so small, a child. I start to say her name...

'What are you doing here?' she demands impatiently, 'and what are you doing with that thing?'

Somehow the hammer has not just jumped out of my pocket and into my hand, but now my hand is raised above my head. I feel repulsed and for a second I want to drop it on the grass, blame the tool for my actions.

It's my only protection so I grip it tighter and give her a look I hope says, *oops* not *I was about to crack you with this tool*, and launch into my speech.

'I'm here about last night. Don't you think we should talk?'

'Why?' she asks almost incredulous, 'It's got nothing to do with you.'

'Nothing to do with me?' I feel drunk on this distortion. 'You accuse me of *this* and then say it's nothing to do with me?' why is it I just can't get the R word out?

'Accuse you of what? Of coming to my house and waving some big spiky thing in my face?' I look at her, both of us confused and then I realise it's because all the time I've been talking I've been gesturing in increasingly wide circles with the hammer. It probably looked like I was swinging for her.

'It's a hammer,' I tell her, 'a claw hammer. You use it for woodwork.'

'What?'

I want to tell her that it's a really decent one too, even if it seems to want to put itself in her little bird shell of a skull, but I know if I don't bring up the R word we could be here all night, or at least until her family come to chop me up and hide me in the antique tea chest.

'I'm here about the rape.' I sounds like I'm a door salesman or something and I know it. *Morning Madam, here about the rape.*

'What are my chances?'

'Oh Charlie,' she laughs nervously and gives me a little shove, 'you didn't do anything wrong.'

And again the world shifts.

Once again I can imagine losing my Virginity to some girl smelling of apples. A girl with a vagina, not a potential birth canal. Most definitely not some guy in a juvenile detentions centre shower block. I am free.

To think I was going to let the hammer bash her.

She's just a girl with some problems. Nothing to do with me. It's like I can't quite believe it, like I half suspected me to have done it too.

'So who was it?'

With mock patience Katie tells me how after I'd left Michael came to see her. Yes, Michael, her brother.

He stood in the doorway of their parent's bedroom waiting to be asked in. He'd stroked the patterns in the bedspread, reading the textures like Braille until his hands had travelled to her body.

These are her words, not mine.

No one has ever stroked anything of mine like they were reading Braille.

She tells me how the whole room glowed and the air was electric and I feel embarrassed that to me it had just seemed stuffy. The whole thing sounds kind of nice, kind of beautiful, if you forget the bit about them sharing the same mummy and daddy. Katie was happy, happy that he held an interest in her, his sister. She wouldn't be pushed away anymore. She wouldn't be forgotten.

It goes on. He had come to her, it was her he wanted. She was special. That Christmas morning she had sat at the breakfast table tracing her fingers across the shells of duck eggs wishing for her brother's skin, now here he was. What a present!

Katie went on to say she knew that if Michael saw the two of us together then he would be provoked into finding her. He would not be able to stand the thought of someone like me inside her.

I wanted to stop and ask her what exactly was wrong with someone like me, the cross-dressing immigrant, but this was certainly her fifteen minutes and she had earned them.

Everyone knew my fucked up wish to be a girl, so she played me and *it was kind of a gift to me to go along with it wasn't it?*

Yeah, thanks Katie.

They kissed, she said, her little fragile body against his. Still sore from her experience with me, they kissed and she felt like she was drowning, maybe she was. But two young siblings in their parents' bed is never an easy thing to be.

And I'm thinking, *do all girls talk like this?*

So with her hand in his, and slightly more entwined than that, she asked him to stop. Were they using any contraception? *No.*

I asked her was it the fear of pregnancy and she looked honestly shocked. How could she ever turn down the opportunity to create a living thing that would glue her and Michael together forever?

I wasn't willing to point out they were already sharing the gene pool intimately enough.

Why then? Fear of revulsion from her parents? *Perhaps* she says.

She has a heavy purple mark on her left cheek and I realise that could have been a present from me or Michael, I don't know.

They didn't stop. She thought it was his weight on her causing her to feel breathless. She thought it was love making her dizzy.

Time moved on and the party below continued without its hosts. A third time she asked him to stop.

'*TeenGirl* magazine says that if he hasn't stopped after asking him to three times then definitely counts as rape.'

My jaw is hanging open by this point, something I always thought was reserved for cartoons. A bug could fly in and I wouldn't notice.

She tilts her head and asks, 'Have you ever asked a man to stop having sex with you just before they're about to come? I guess not.'

I want to retaliate with some sharp comment to shut her up, tell her that you don't ask men to stop when they're paying you or something, let her know I've tasted the real world. But I bite my tongue and shake my head.

'It doesn't work.' She pauses to let this sink in.

'Oh' I say, as if I care.

'So I screamed,' she shrugs casually, 'I screamed and screamed until-' I wait for her to say *I'm sick* but it doesn't come, '-until I couldn't hear anything else. When I stopped screaming I couldn't hear the music from the party. I thought maybe I'd gone deaf from the shock or something. I've read that can happen, when you're shocked. Then my parents bust in and Dad rips Michael off me, I don't remember much after that.'

She looks at me, all big numb eyes and behind them a fucked-up brain.

She's waiting for a response but she's asking for a lot, and she isn't really what I'm focusing on because in this moment I think I'm first experiencing freedom.

I know for sure now. I am not a criminal. I am not one of the bad guys.

I start to notice how crisp and sharp the night air is and how it stings if you breathe in deeply enough.
I notice how her shoulders are covered in tiny goose pimples, how I can't ever remember seeing a goose. How the hammer's rubber handle is so warm and clammy it feels like someone's skin clenching tightly to my own.

And how even though I am so alone right now, so very far away from home, from normal, somewhere in the universe is Matka, sending out these sharp rays of unconditional love. I am loved.

And I am not responsible for scrunching up Katie's mental state.

This sense of freedom is something that I think about a lot later on. Such a powerful feeling wasted on this evening.

'Well?' Katie snaps, 'What do you think now, hey?'

For a second I see her as I think she actually is, a manipulative little bitch so full of venom it makes my mouth ache just thinking about her. Isn't this the feeling all men have about women?

'You're nuts.' I tell her, 'Grade-A fruit loop.'

'And?'

'What do you want me to say Katie?'

I'm sorry you've joined the legions of the fucked up? I'm sorry your parents will resent the both of you every time they see your faces?

This is a rollercoaster of emotion all right and she is strapped in right next to me.

I want to get out of here, just run like every man and women in every black and white horror film before me, just get the fuck away and forget about it.

Suddenly I feel very tired.

She's still there, hovering over me, the waiting slowly fading the longer I stay silent. But I know she's never going to just disappear.

Our eyes meet properly for the first time. An onlooker would be forgiven for mistaking this as a lover's tiff.

She's looks hurt at my lack of response, although I'm sure she'd be more hurt if she could hear my thoughts.

Hey Katie, how about:

I'm sorry you've gotten Michael castrated?
I'm sorry your parents are in the backyard burning the sheets?
I'm sorry this is all your fault?

Still nothing comes out of my mouth. Her bottom lip starts to quiver and I think she's going to cry. So it's another act, but it's one I fall for.

'Look, Katie, sorry about what happened okay? It's just…'

Then I crack. There on the grass I crack.

My feet wet through my trainers, my dirty bike lying on their perfect lawn, like two secret lovers we cry. I cannot protect her from this, I cannot offer her anything but this. The girl is messed up. We hold each other, angry and brittle. She cries, I cry. I put my arm around her, and cry out harshly for relief.

She thinks it's for her but its entirely selfish.

We are shallow. Katie is broken and I can't fix her because I am too busy trying to fix myself.

God, I'm a teenage boy with blackouts who masquerades as a girl. I don't have time for anyone else's shit.

No matter how bad things are for her right now, no matter how unbearable, all I can think about is that it wasn't me that raped her.

I am not my Papa.

Exhausted and intoxicated with relief I just want to go to cycle home to bed, but I can't. I'm still on this lawn, still with Katie and her weight in my arms is my responsibility, if only for this moment.

In a funny way I feel like I've lost something.

For twelve hours I had been a rapist at fourteen. I made changes in the faces and voices of people I met.

The people I knew forgot about their problems and began to worry about the living problem standing in front of them.

The words on their lips were not of their sob stories, not of God or even Katie. They were of me.

I stroke Katie's hair gently with the head of the hammer, the claw shining against the moonlight, my hands still gripped around the rubber.

I say soothing words, explain things could be worse.

She asks how and I tell her about a party I once went to dressed as a girl. When I got there most of the people had moved downstairs into a basement.

I stood in the kitchen wondering where everyone was while reapplying a thick layer of mascara until some kid walked passed with a joint in his hand.

I followed him and as I got nearer to the basement door you could hear all this manic shouting and thrash music like someone was trying to mask it.

I mean who listens to thrash music anyway? This isn't the eighties.

I walked around for a bit, thought about going home, but I knew Papa would be in. There was nothing else to do but go down there.

In the corner was an old furnace that smelt a bit like it had been used to barbeque some cheap fatty meat – the kind you get at the low price foreign hypermarkets, the kind where we shop.

I'd been to some pretty rancid places but it smelt so bad down there, sweat and piss and flesh – underneath it all the time that awful scorched smell – like when you singe your hair on a cigarette.

There must have been forty maybe fifty boys and a quarter as many girls in a huge circle.

I thought it was a mosh pit at first, then I saw. In the centre there was a girl in her underwear, maybe seventeen years old.

Someone had tied her up and a couple of the boys were jabbing her with bits of heated metal. Later I found out they were mostly crowbars and a few gardening tools.

This girl lying in her own piss, being branded like a cow was now puking and convulsing hysterically. The stench of her searing flesh filled the basement. Who would think kids were capable of such things?

'I had to get out of there,' I tell Katie, 'it was torture.'

'I guess that is worse,' she says, weighing it against her own predicament when she's decided this girl suffered more than her she adds, 'but why would anyone do such a thing?'

'Don't know, maybe she just fucked with the wrong person.' After saying this I smile sweetly.

The story is wasted, she isn't scared of what could happen to her when she gets Michael sent off to mental rehabilitation. She's scared of what has already happened, not what lies ahead.

'Is that story even real?' she asks.

'Nah,' I say, admitting defeat, 'it's just some video I saw on the Junked.com.'

I think then that I've added my share of damage to Katie and still it's less than if I'd have been the one to rape her.

It's the right time for me to leave and there's this tiny part of me that's smug to have gotten out of what seemed to be the worst thing that could ever happen to a boy, but as it turns out this is just the beginning, this is where it all started to go wrong for me.

'I've got to go, sorry about all this.' I say shrugging my shoulders and nearly hitting her with the hammer.

She nods, wiping snot from her nose with her sleeve. Her eyes half close and she goes to kiss me, but I stop her.

'Sorry Katie, I don't do girls anymore,' I lie.

MIKE

Home is a bedroom in a converted basement of a council house. It's a set of neon stencils on my concrete grey walls: a moon, a heart, a star.

Home is warm and safe and quiet.

Home is not having bruises on your ribs from your parents beating you or in Michael Rowan's case, not having your sister seduce you. Where's he going to go now?

Home for me is a window touching my ceiling with weeds poking through the warped frame.

If you are willing to risk grass stains over your body then you can climb through my bedroom window and into my bed.

Green tribal streaks smeared across your chest mark your heroic journey across the communal lawn, which is yellowing in patches and littered with many a dangerous stray kitty.

That's where I find myself tonight, heading back to my bedroom, dark and safe and warm.

But when I climb through my window I become downsized very quickly because tonight I am a visitor in my own room.

Papa is sitting on the rumpled bed and he's staring at my vest covered in green streaks. His hammer, the one Matka warned me against taking, is still gripped in my hand.

'Now I just can't believe you needed to hammer something out on the lawn at half past five in the morning,' Papa says and I can't tell if it's a joke or if he's about to hit me.

I know he must be lying about the time, I look at my Casio. 0536. He's right. I've lost hours.

And what is Papa doing here, in the house that used to be ours and now is mine.

I can't remember how long he's been away, but it looks like he's grown too large for my room, too massive for this house that is already crammed full with Matka and me.

There is nothing here for him.

'Does Matka know you're here?' is all I can think of to ask, trying desperately to even the balance of power but my voice sounds flat.

He's wearing an overall and it's caked in layer after layer of brown and black dust. I don't ask what it is; it's really not my place to ask him.

'Do you really care what your mother thinks Charlie? Do you think *I* care if she knows I'm talking to you now? You are my son, you know.' he says *son* but I hear *possession*.

There's a thick line of stubble making a tiny landscape across his chin. I focus on it to avoid looking into his eyes.

'I guess not.'

'Well then, come and sit next to me and tell me what you were doing with my hammer,' he says, gently patting the bed. I sit down beside him on my low mattress.

The covers have been pulled back and I try to avoid looking at the stains on the sheets.

Papa strokes my hair that used to be brown and is now a washed-out blonde.

He runs his fingers through the extensions pushing open the knots until he reaches where my hair ends just above my spine.

His hand lingers there for a second and I can feel the warmth of his skin resting against the gap of flesh between my vest and trousers. I don't move at all, as if keeping still means he won't be able to reach me.

The heat of his body still feels like anger and he moves his hand away.

He asks about the hammer, so I tell him.

I tell him about the party, about screwing Katie. I miss out the parts about my dressing as a girl and my memory lapse but focus instead on the suspected rape charges because I know he'll like that bit.

As I talk the word VIRGINITY flashes up in front of my eyes in bright white lights and I wonder for a second if the story had finished differently, if I had slept with her, if it was me she'd wanted, then I might feel like a different person now, being someone that had had sex.

Normal boy-girl sex.

I tell Papa how I don't really know what I was planning to do with the hammer, hit her maybe, scare her more likely. His expression is blank and I wonder for a moment if I'd been talking at all or just imagining it. He is looking through me.

After a moment's hesitation I finish by telling him it wasn't me at all but her brother, Michael, and at this he creaks to life, laughing in huge bellows from the pit of his stomach like Michael is a human punchline.

Like everything I do is trivial and it could never rouse anything but amusement in him. Like Katie's whole fucked-up life is just one big sketch to make him laugh.

Within seconds I don't care about any of that, I just want him to quieten down so he doesn't wake Matka. I don't know what she'd do if she knew he was here.

We're back to the silence until he decides its lesson time and soon Papa is telling me there are victims in this world, you can learn to sense them, *smell* them with some primal sense.

They are everywhere; on buses, in the mysterious workplace that I have not yet experienced, in public toilets and market stands.

I nod, I've heard this one before. I know it's my job to look alert and be thankful for the information he's giving me. I try to smile even when I feel my dry lips crack open and warm blood fill the creases.

But tonight there is more, something new. He tells me of a man in the factory where he now works, a man who is a victim. I stare at Papa's name badge, sewn on his uniform. Our family name, Lewandoski, is too long and instead there are just four letters, LEWD. A joke, perhaps.

'Never be a victim Charlie. Matka is a victim and look at her. Women usually are. She didn't start off that way - she used to be strong and proud.' He pauses to breathe in deeply, 'then she met me, now she's a shadow, a mouse scratching at the surface of my memory, creeping across my thoughts trying to remain unnoticed. Even the weak are noticed and when they are you know you've found a victim.' The words sound rehearsed, but if they're meant to panic me, they work.

I never get to hear the full story of the man at the factory, all I know is that he did something to upset Papa and he paid for it. Before the details come he's onto something else.

He's telling me it is good for him to work at the factory – his strength has increased threefold. He could pick Matka up with one hand.

I imagine that he wants to compare himself to some Greek mythological character but he can't think of one. Papa may be many things, but he's not academic.

He asks some questions, general stuff about school, exams, the English award. All easy ones I know the answers to. My nerves are settling with each minute.

He tells me if anyone tries to hurt me then he'll track them down and beat them to death.

I wonder vaguely if a person can beat themselves to death. An image of him in our kitchen trying to hit himself with a pan sends a warm fuzz into my brain and for a few seconds I almost miss him.

Almost.

Finally, as the sun starts to rise and I feel tired to the point of nausea I summon the blind courage to ask him what I want to know.

'Where did you go, Papa? I mean where did you move to?'

He doesn't say anything at first, just looks at me as if I am mad to ask him questions. I guess he's still Charlie the Conqueror. He grabs my face and squishes my cheeks so hard the insides of my mouth touch together.

He breaks away and there's a flurry of demands between us, like, whoever breaks the questions loses.

'When is Matka next taking you to the doctors?'

'How do you know I'm still going?'

'What's that supposed to mean?'

A pause from me while I try to work out another question to respond with.

'Answer,' he states.

'Day after my birthday.' I reply, hoping he won't remember when that is.

'Do you think I've forgotten when you were born?'

'No.' I think about making it sound like a question but it's not worth it. I have years to learn how to beat him at these games, tonight I am just tired.

'Then shut up. How could I forget? You were enough bloody trouble.' He means my birth. Matka nearly died from blood loss.

She likes to tell people I was her most treasured gift and greatest trial. The doctors back in Poland had to remove her womb afterward, so no brother or sister.

She says here, in England, that wouldn't have happened. Now my birthday is also a day we celebrate Matka surviving pushing me out of her birth canal, and living through it.

We'll talk more about it after your birthday,' he says.

Neither of us knows it yet, but by my birthday I'll have met someone who is stronger than him.

Nothing is said after that for a long time.

Somewhere in the silence, he goes back to touching my hair, softly at first in long dramatic strokes, then harder, his hand touching my forehead and pulling the weight of his arm over my head and down my back, tugging at my skin.

Finally, as if bored with my stillness he grabs the hair by the nape of my neck and clutching his coarse fingers around it he says to me:

'I like long hair Charlie, I like it a lot, just not on you. So cut it off.'

Exit father, enter sleep.

The Ford is parked outside before my Casio clicks around to 0800 hours. I've got a duffle bag and tea flask with me, inside the bag is a blue dress Jack's sister donated to the Charlie Lewandowski eveningwear collection, all the change lying around the house and my lucky broken socket wrench.

Today it is a weapon. I feel like I need something heavy to swipe at anyone who gets too close.

I open the fridge and the chill hits me, I always feel like I am burning up after coming face to face with Papa. The man is like radiation.

I down half a pint of semi skimmed and use the carton to weigh down a note I've left for Matka saying I'm spending a few days at Jack's house.

I think about explaining that Papa visited, which probably means she left the kitchen door unlocked, but in the end I just leave it out and try to make up for my absence by adding a string of xoxox's after my name.

The x's are kisses, the o's, hugs.

As soon as I hit the passenger seat, things begin to feel better. Jack is in his dressing gown and when his feet move to the different peddles the flaps of his gown fall open revealing brown hairy legs and a pair of soiled blue Wellingtons.

He catches my eye, laughs and says, 'Well you said you were in a hurry. This is me getting here in a hurry.'

Last year he didn't have the Ford, it still belonged to his sister Judy, but she got into some debt and ended up selling it to him on the cheap. I've never been so grateful for someone else's misfortune. I can't imagine cycling to Jack's house this morning.

He asks about the trouble with Papa and I keep it vague, it's not something I like going over. I say he appeared out the blue and bothered me. Jack raises an eyebrow but I don't bite. For now that will have to do.

Jack's parents are still sitting at the breakfast table in their kitchen when I return. Next to them is Judy. Her skin is yellow and sagging. I can see the sweat sitting on her forehead.

I know she's only twenty-two but some days she looks like she's fifty or something. In front of her is a bowl of orange and white slush that was probably cornflakes and milk about an hour ago.

'Judy's got the flu,' Jack's dad announces as we sit down at the table.

Judy has had the flu for as long as I've known her. Outside their house Judy has a nasty heroin habit, but when you're sitting with their parents, Judy has the flu.

I've never seen anyone on heroin but Judy and I don't need to as she pretty much looks like the poster girl for why you shouldn't send your kids away to university. Or let them leave the house.

Despite looking like she's dead, she seems to take it pretty well, lolling about the house in an old dressing gown, her long brown hair held in place by grease.

She'll play Connect Four with you if you ask her and when she's in the mood she'll get her old photo album out and you can see she was beautiful before as well, just in a different way. Now I'm wearing women's clothes, I might make her my fashion muse.

Jack's red plastic pager starts to dance across the table. The family watch it for two seconds, then three, all held by its vibration. For a moment I think it could be Matka, which is ridiculous, really. The pager is for Jack's business. His arm reaches out and then snaps it up. He puts it in his pocket without reading the message.

He told me the business started when Judy came back from university. She was messed up in a big way and he wanted to help out so Jack began dealing grass at college to help pay for her addiction. They were both sure their parent's wouldn't find out if they were careful. Eventually they did. Even our generation can't watch *Sesame Street* repeats eight hours a day for a year without someone asking questions.

The buzz of the pager is ignored, just a rustle of the paper from Jack's dad and then it's back to playing happy families. His mother's mouth twitches tightly and I try not to smile at her. I wonder if she finds me attractive.

So here's what we do. Jack pulls some clothes on and we jump into the Ford, three of us this time. Judy comes along for the ride and I ask if she wants to sit in the front, this did used to be her car after all - but she just smiles so widely it looks like she's got an orange quarter in there and climbs onto the back seat.

We drive to a local patch of shops and Jack picks up some whisky and Coke. The car growls into life and just when the reggae tape is ready to loop Judy finds one of her old cassettes down the back of her seat. Dutifully I take it from her and slide it into the little dark rectangle, waiting to hear who Judy used to be.

A woman with the kind of voice that sounds like she's singing through warm, wet velvet is jerking a song out of the speakers that moments before had Eddy Grant bumping the Ford along.

The woman is singing about a beauty queen, a ring, a car, never getting where she wants to be. Judy's eyes are closed nodding to the music. She strokes the rough fake leather upholstery, calls the Ford *baby* and coos to it whenever it sounds like it might stall.

Judy sings, asking if we'll kiss for her. I wonder if Judy is the most perfect woman I've ever seen, her lips syncing to the words of a song that belonged to her when she was whole, riding in the back of her old car, kid brother and friend tagging along.

She seems more content than anyone else I know and I run a checklist through my head of people I love and she wins the best life award hands down. She's like a cat that just sits around sleeping and zoning into another place all day.

I wish that it were summer, then her skin might be brown instead of yellow and this moment would be perfect. Judy sings that she may find herself delayed.

We pull into the petrol station and while Jack is paying, Judy calls me into the women's toilet. She rifles through my bag, desperate for a moment, searching for something and it's no good me asking what it is she wants because I'm not sure she knows herself.

The contents of my duffle spill onto the filthy, once white tiles of the toilet floor. Judy pounces on an item but when I lean nearer, I see it's just her old dress.

Somehow I don't think this was what she's been searching for. But then the muscles in her face animate and I realise she's smiling.

'I went to my college leaving party in this dress. I kissed Thom Saunders in this dress.' She throws it at me.

'Put it on.' I do.

She's combing my hair with her fingers when Jack knocks on the heavy door. Judy calls for him to come in, like this is a beauty parlour not a roadside shithouse. 'You look great,' she tells me. 'Doesn't he look great, Jack?'

'Hot,' he says, 'now, can we get back in the car?' but Judy doesn't want to go just yet, she's remembered what she's looking for and as I try to pile the items back in the bag she pulls them back out, like a puppy that isn't sure if it's being cute or annoying.

'Saint Bernards slobber too much.' I announce to the room.

Judy finds a thick black pen, the kind kids are always sniffing in class, hoping the faint toxins will destroy their boredom for minutes at a time.

'We'll teach him,' she whispers to me and I like the feeling of belonging to something private, a joke for just the two of us.

The cap comes off and she scrawls hurriedly on the wall, first a number, then a message but I don't stop to read either of them because outside, the hum of the Ford is calling and Jack is getting impatient.

We take Judy home, I don't want to do it but Jack explains it's for her own good, so she's safe inside before it's time for her next dose. She's like a zombie or a vampire with a curfew.

Back at their house she gets out of the Ford and pauses before going inside. I want her to turn back, tap on the window and plant a kiss on my cheek but when she turns to look back I realise it's the Ford Cortina and its lifetime of memories she is interested in, not us.

We drive around all afternoon waiting for something to happen, wasting petrol and wasting time. Jack lets me have a quick spin in one of the old supermarket car parks. I'm getting pretty good at driving now, I can take corners and once I reversed between two of those huge recycling bins. It'll be years before I'm old enough to buy a car, but I want to be able to drive perfectly and take my test the day I turn seventeen.

Hopefully in three years I'll have saved enough to buy myself a car and drive out of this town forever. I know it's not original, but everyone needs an exit strategy.

This evening my plans are no more concrete than to have my wallet filled by the time the sun comes up. I'll do what it takes, from lifting things from the 24-7 to grabbing some rich woman's purse. Hell, once we even stole a pedigree dog. It shit all over the car so we left it on the hard shoulder. Boys will be boys.

And if this place is supposed to be safer than anywhere for miles, it doesn't seem that way with us around.

We reel down the windows of the Ford and let the cold air rush through the car and feed the adrenaline that's needed if we're going to do what we're going to do.

It's important to remember it's not easy getting money when you're fourteen and live in a concrete block.

If this were a film then I'd be cruising a rich housewife in her forties.

She would be watching me mow the lawn with my shirt off and slipping twenty pound notes into the back of my jeans pocket at the end of the evening. I'd be giving dance lessons and dipping my hands in their waistbands.

We're out the car and walking up a suburban street, looking for something that catches our attention. I can't explain it better than that. You just learn to spot an opportunity, sometimes you smell it on the air, other times you see a crack in the woodwork, an open gate, a lorry unloading goods with a driver out of sight, three pints of milk on a doorstep that have curdled in a week's worth of sun.

We get to a big detached house, with an elaborate gravel drive. It's at the end of the road, pretty quiet and all the lights are off.

I've never actually broken into a house before, I don't think Jack has either, not sober anyway.

In my mind there's this song, it sometimes comes into my head when we're doing this kind of thing, like it keeps me moving. It's something from an old film, like danger music. It starts off really quiet, but then it just builds and builds until a whole orchestra is egging us on, and the music is right there with us, protecting us almost.

How can we possibly go back now?

We edge around the back of the house in stealth mode, hands touching the walls, bodies snagging against the mortar, just like the films.

Jack is so close to me I can feel his body heat, even through his hoodie, which is now up. My heart is pumping so fast it feels like it's trying to bounce out of my chest and into my throat.

I hold my breath because it seems too loud and it just keeps coming in big wheezy gasps, but the noise is not from my lungs. I turn to Jack but he's looking into the back garden, hand clasped over his mouth. So it's not his breathing either.

I can't see a thing so I keep perfectly still, remaining in the shadow of the house where I like to think it's safe. Time drifts in and out of shape and Jack still stares at whatever it is I can't see.

It's the chill that finally shakes me into focus. I'm still wearing the dress and my balls are shrinking to the size of walnuts. I bet if I had been brought up in Poland like Papa they'd have hardened from the cold by now.

The music in my head has died completely and I've still not seen anything and I guess my concentration drops and I start to smooth the gravel path with my foot.

Jack turns around at the noise and pulls an expression for me to stop. His face comes closer to mine.

'Shut up, she'll hear you,' he hisses at me. So there's a woman, somewhere on the other side of the wall, or in the back of the garden. Wherever she is she is near enough to hear us, it's probably her property we're on.

My balls feel even tighter. I'm sure we're trapped.

Just then his pager goes off. It buzzes once, then twice from the pocket of his jeans. We both know if he doesn't get to it by the third buzz a metallic rendition of *No Woman, No Cry* will blast out into the night.

Jack fumbles quickly, his hands delving frantically into his pockets, dropping a baggie on the floor, cursing under his breath.

The dim green of the pager appears in his hands but it's too late. The first two bars play before he can activate the button to shut the thing up.

A small rectangle of light has appeared on the grass in what seems like a direct response to the pager and we both flinch, hunched up like kids in that stupid game where you have to keep still when the music stops.

Which is what this is I guess.

The wheezing continues and Jack guides me to his position, the gravel unstable beneath our feet, crunching noisily and threatening to expose our whereabouts with each movement.

The light comes from a utility room, a squat block that looks like it was fitted onto the house as an afterthought.

Inside are several smaller white blocks like a washer, a dryer, a freezer.

Still I hear the wheezing, too irregular to be one of the machines, too husky, too wet. Too *Saint Bernard*.

At that moment I see possibly the sickest sight my fourteen year old eyes have witnessed. It's a woman. Maybe 70. She's folding up blankets or sheets or something then balancing them on the side. She's doing this all naked, completely naked. Her tits point straight down like misfired rockets, guiding her body toward the laundry.

Every now and then she lifts up another batch and that's the wheezing noise, her heaving the weight of the blankets back up. It almost makes me want to step out of the shadows and help, just to stop her from doing it.

The first time I caught her on the way up and that wasn't as grim, just a load of leathery pale skin on a hunched up frame but when she went to duck back down, I felt the laughter rise up in me.

This is the woman Jack has been watching for the past five minutes. Just an old woman, doing her laundry naked.

Thirty years ago her body would have been hot.

Thirty years ago I wasn't born.

The noise of my, and now Jack's, laughter makes her look up and peer into the darkness of the garden, but of course now she's turned the light on she can only see her own reflection.

I half imagine her coming out into the garden, her bare feet on the damp grass, her nipples getting hard for the first time in years.

She doesn't come out, what she does do is pick up a cordless phone and start to dial. Our cue to exit.

We run, not at all quietly across the gravel and a neighbour's security light goes on making Jack run into the road where a white van speeds past nearly knocking him down.

We look at each other, feeling alive after a near miss at death. The music is back and it's pulsing through my body, hitting hard in my ears and my heart telling me we're clearly invincible. After all, an old lady hasn't caught us and Jack hasn't been hit by a van.

This night will be a good one, I can feel it.

Our luck isn't over yet, because when we reach the corner of the road, a police car crawls to meet us. I think they're going to stop and ask questions but the driver, a small fat lady officer just tips her head at us and we nod back – all foolish grins and goofy walks.

I think about the baggie on the path and decide not to mention it to Jack, he's got more than enough gear and I don't want to be the one who has to go back and get it.

Why spoil a perfect exit?

Back at the Ford, breathless and cackling we decide to hit the motorway.

Our new found exhilaration fills the air of the car until I'm so wired I have to sit on my hands to stop throwing out little shadow boxing moves.

Jack reads the pager message that nearly got us caught then checks his watch. He turns off the cassette tape as we speed along the tarmac, blurring the other vehicles as we thrash them in a race they don't know they've entered.

It isn't until we take the turn off that I realise where the car is heading.

We're speeding toward a rundown estate that was built in the sixties, a concrete mass of houses, factories and shops all made to the same design. It was abandoned by anyone with money, sense and a visa, when my neighbourhood was built. It makes my part of town look like *Disneyland*.

Matka has always made out that the place was filled with bad people. To keep me away she gave me the impression that all the men had coarse hands from a life of brawling and beating their wives and all the women walked funny as they were so poor they would most likely be selling their bodies, or their children or their children's bodies.

The trouble is, I'm pretty sure she's right and I don't like the idea of spending our money-making evening on the estate because in a place like that, when it comes to it, under all the dirt and scum people will only exchange their money for the worst of things.

We pass the disused bowling alleys and bars and a pornographic cinema Jack and I snuck into a few summers back with glowing neon lights that burn the outlines of women onto your eyes.

We pass disused warehouses and factories where the poor and the unfortunate slave long into the night only to sleep for a few precious hours and then return for the day shift.

The only actual people I see are a boy wearing a long leather coat, the kind you use to hide a big gun, lightly kiss a Japanese girl goodbye on the corner of Saint Augustine Road, the patron saint of brewers. I can't imagine what they've been doing; there is nothing to do here.

Then the Ford turns down Marlowe Road and onto a path I don't know and the couple, like all other things outside the car seem to disappear into the night until finally, passing the abandoned church, I glimpse two homeless men walking the night away.

We are in the staff parking lot of a factory that Jack tells me makes custard creams and bourbon biscuits. 'Your favourite,' he says, 'must be a lucky sign.'

We sit inside the car with the engine still running and the headlights glaring in front of us. Jack tells me when we open the doors, the sweet scent of biscuits will hit my nose instantly and no matter how strong it seems at first, if we stay here for longer than fifteen minutes I won't even be able to notice it. That'll be our sign to leave, when we can't smell the biscuits anymore.

'What's the plan?' I ask, and he gives me this sorry little expression, almost a shrug of an apology. 'The plan is to make some money. I've been here before, it's nothing you can't handle.'

Before I can ask anything else, a man raps his knuckles on the passenger window and we both jump at the sound. 'Remember. Cash up front,' says Jack and he steps out the car.

The last of the fire that burned inside me so fiercely earlier is pissed out when I open the door of the car and step on a split rubber.

That sick sweet smell hits my nostrils just as Jack predicted and the cold air lifts a hundred goose pimples up on my arms.

The man who knocked on the window looks me up and down and nods to his two friends who are standing in the shadows behind him. I am going to be sick.

We stand a few feet apart, watching each other and I keep trying to think of another reason Jack would have brought me here, but the inevitable conclusion keeps getting closer and closer until it feels like it's choking me and there's nothing I can do about it.

I don't think it counts if you lose the big V this way.

A whistle sounds from somewhere within the factory and men and a few women pour like ants out of a small side door. I actually sigh with relief.

But the few with cars leave quickly, and the rest walk across the tarmac and into the night. No one comes over to ask what we're doing. I look around for someone to call out to or a car to give me a lift home. Nothing. The Ford is easily one of the better cars in the lot. I guess the biscuit business doesn't bring home much cash.

The two friends of the first man step forward, as they move nearer the dark spaces where their heads should be are replaced by yellowing features. I guess the men are of Papa's generation, I wonder if they know him or someone like him and as each moment passes I am sure they must -

one of them even looks Polish. These men could be Papa's friends, brothers, comrades, uncles at my childhood birthday parties. That doesn't help me one bit.

Breathing deeply, staring at these strangers, I think of warnings, something to trigger my senses and make me run but I'm frozen to the spot and nothing comes. I can't even turn around to look at Jack.

Would things be different if I hadn't been wearing a dress? I bring my head down and beneath the strong sick smell of biscuits I catch a waft of my perfume.

Just that tiny memory of home is enough to get me through what is coming next. I wish I'd worn more, but it belongs to Matka and she notices when I take it. Then I'm wondering is she awake right now?

The man coughs to hurry things along and from behind me Jack says something I don't hear. I know now that whatever they want I'll do, as long as we can leave as soon as it's over and it means when I wake up in the morning my wallet will be full, even if my heart is empty.

Twenty minutes pass and with it the smell of biscuits. I'm still here, on my knees for the third time, and the gravel is tearing my tights, leaving tiny speckles of grit imprinted on my shins. He waited and watched his two friends first, probably making sure I wouldn't do anything crazy, like bite.

I keep thinking of the money and how it will one day turn into a sleek black tire of a car registered in my name driving me out of this town forever. But the back of my neck is hot and sticky where this Polish fucker, probably even a Catholic, is weighing his heavy hands. *Don't worry mister, mother Mary loves you, she'll forgive you come Sunday.*

I can feel the sweat from his hands mingle with the sweat of my neck, this somehow is worse than his cock pushed deep against my throat.

This isn't easy money. It can't ever be easy unless maybe you are high first and then you'd have to be a total smack head to be able to cope. But it is money, and easier in a way than that heart pumping fear of robbing someone when you're just as shit scared as they are, hoping they don't notice the knife in your hand shaking, not even knowing how much you're going to get for your hard work.

This is money and then it is time passing, always passing. Every second bringing me closer to finishing, to a full wallet, a future without Papa and a chance to kick Jack until I rupture his spleen for getting me into this.

I promise myself when this is over, I won't let it keep me awake at night, I'd rather spend an eternity sucking old men off in the back of factories than be the one pumping some young boy dressed as a girl.

I ask you all who is the pathetic one? Not me.

Not me. I'm just a kid.

These men aren't going to go home to their wives or their dogs and wonder how a good kid like me got into this situation, because if they did they wouldn't do this kind of shit.

If this was your only trick you'd have to be desperate, money to the mafia desperate. Far from home desperate. Maybe that's it?

Maybe these people think they can do this to me because there is no one worrying about me, about Jack. But there is someone worrying about me and she's waiting at home.

Home is a concrete council house protecting the woman who gave me life.

Then suddenly I see her in my mind, Matka sitting at the kitchen table, crying. She's clutching the local newspaper, a story about a kid found dead in a factory car park and the pages are scrunched tight in her tiny fists which are raised to her chest.

And then I see nothing.

I taste the imitation leather that makes up the backseat of the Cortina, my face pushed down into the creases and cracks. Those rough little cracks scraping my forehead have worn in over time; they map out memories that belong to other people, memories that mean more than this one will.

'Stay with me Charlie,' Jack calls. It's comforting, the kind of words you'd expect from a paramedic. I focus on his eyes in the rear view mirror and try to gage how badly things have gone from his expression.

'Did we get the money?' I ask and he confirms, yes, the money is in our possession. I wait for the blanks to fill themselves in, but already I know they are not going to come.

'Good,' I tell him, 'because I'm going to have you for this.' I push my head down further, gulping the muggy air in big heaving lungfuls. For now it could taste of shit and it'd be better than being back in that car park.

A dull, blinding headache is creeping into my skull so when Jack tells me I have a right to be angry and it's fair enough I should get to pound him a little I don't bother to respond.

Inside my head I call him any name I can think of, focusing all of my energy on my anger and away from the pain that is building every time I take another breath.

We swerve around a corner and a wave of nausea builds up from the lining of my stomach and burns all the way up my throat.

I wonder if the violent swing of the car was deliberate but before I can decide another one comes, setting my throat muscles into spasms. I open my mouth and out shoots a gush of hot, stinking vomit.

'Sorry, thought I saw a police car,' Jack explains. As we pull up at a traffic light he turns his head around to look at me and the puke that now covers the back seat and most of the window. Even with just the streetlights, we can both see the vomit is the wrong colour.

'Is that blood?' he says and the look on his face tells me he suddenly feels out of his depth. It tells me he's thinking about what to say to the police if I die in the back of his car.

'I think I need a hospital,' I tell him.

When I was five or six, I went to hospital to have a lump removed from my throat. Matka sat patiently drawing cats and dogs and birds with me as she tried to push the word CANCER to the back of her mind and blank out her face.

Papa waited in the car.

After the operation the pain was so great I thought it was a punishment for an undiscovered crime I had committed, some childhood version of karma.

My parents explained that I'd done nothing wrong and even if I had, then any physical pain I was experiencing wasn't a direct consequence of that.

I never doubted either of them then, not the mouse or the monster. Now I am starting to think they were wrong.

Jack reaches for the play button on the tape player but his fingers slide off it and the radio comes on instead.

We listen to Janet Jackson repeating again and again a chorus to an old Joni Mitchell song until I begin to wonder if somehow it is a tape and she's on a constant loop.

But it slows Jack's driving and her voice is kind of hypnotic and I begin to close my eyes, just for seconds at a time and then longer.

I open them again when Jack hits the stereo and I realise he's desperate for Janet Jackson to shut up. His curls are pushed behind his ears and his wet cheeks shine under the passing streetlights. Janet just keeps on singing and Jack wipes his face with the back of his hoodie sleeve, then very calmly presses the off button on the stereo. We're back to silence.

'Will you tell them you're my next of kin?' I ask, knowing what will happen if either of my parents are called to the hospital.

'What?'

'At the hospital, will you lie and say I'm your brother or something? So my parents aren't called.'

'Charlie, we can't go to the hospital. What will we tell them?' When it comes to the turn off for the hospital Jack speeds the car up ignores the sign. I don't say anything, there's nothing I can say. We hit the short passage of motorway taking us home, or as close as home can be.

Our eyes meet in the rear view mirror.

'You could just drop me off at A and E. Pulp Fiction style. You don't have to wait.'

'Dude, you'll be fine,' he tells me, 'it's not that bad. I promise I'm going to sort you out.' Somehow, I believe him. I have to.

I can feel the motor vibrate beneath me and this sense of comfort is the last thing I remember before my head becomes too heavy to lift and I have to shut my eyes.

The Ford speeds up. The crack of open window allows snippets of sound from the streets.

Other people living other lives and I look for a way to trade places with them, fall into their tracks. I am envious of life.

Time has passed but I don't know how long. The seat peels from my cheek as Jack lifts me up and carries me along the path. I can feel the air against the dampness of my head and it makes me shiver, sending a chill deep into my skull but I don't know if the wet is blood or sweat or vomit maybe.

Jack crunches up a gravel driveway, his footfalls sound heavier under both our weight. His arms hoisting my body higher each time they begin to slip. My eyes are too heavy to open and I can't work out where we are. Not my house, not his.

The doorway opens into a dark living room, Jack lays me onto a smooth velour couch and I watch as he walks toward the warm yellow light leading into the kitchen.

The tiny glow burns onto my eyes each time I try to look at it and when I call out for Jack my voice sounds hoarse and empty. Then the kitchen light firmly clicks off and there is nothing but darkness.

Fingers creeping around my ribs, searching, reaching like they are attempting to lift my wallet. I sit up in the dark, wary of hitting my head against the body attached to the wandering hands.

A light goes on and instinctively my eyes close but I prize them open and in front of me is a woman I've never seen before. She's wearing a light blue uniform, buttoned high to her neck and there's something familiar about her. She presses her fingers harder into my ribs.

'Does that hurt?' she asks and when I don't answer she tries something else. 'Charles? Can you hear me, Charles?' and now her thumbs are over my eyelids, her face half a frown as she peers deep into my pupils.

'He prefers Charlie,' someone says.

I squint to look past the blind patch caused by the lamp light and it's Jack. He's standing at a distance, like I might be infectious, his arms crossed.

Next to him is Barbie. I look at the woman again. Although there's twenty years between them and the woman's hair is brown, not jet black, I can see they are related. It's Barbie's Mum.

'Are you going to take me to the hospital?'

'No, love. I've just come from there. You'll be fine here for now.' She lets out a heavy sigh after her and I realise she must see this kind of thing at work all day long. She doesn't even bother to ask me how it happened; she won't get any truthful answers.

'You can wake me up if he gets worse,' she says to the room and with that she heaves herself up and begins to walk up the stairs. I want to shout after her that we shouldn't wait until I get worse, that I need help now, that I don't even know how I got from the car park to the Ford, that I'm just a kid, but she's gone.

Jack and Barbie remain standing, just out of reach in case I should puke again.

It's only the second time I've seen Barbie close up and she couldn't look more different. Her thick make-up has been wiped off and she's wearing a little nasal strip to help her breathe.

She tells me that she always gets a cough and a cold in the winter. In this half-light she even could seem beautiful, nothing like the slutty girl that earned her name.

Her legs are a little too rounded and her black hair is thick like a modern Egyptian, she even has the stupid fringe. She's wearing a Metallica t-shirt that almost reaches her knees and although this seems strange it's not till I notice her bare feet that I realise we probably got her out of bed.

'Thanks,' I say.

She smiles genuinely and this is something missing in a lot of girls I know. She looks so innocent right now that standing next to Jack, you'd think there was a law against them dating. In fact, the more I think about it, there probably is.

There's been so much shit said about her, how she needs to get off with everyone she meets, just to make some kind of connection, like without a blowjob she isn't going to make a lasting impression.

'I mean thanks for looking after us,' I tell her, 'and thank your parents too, for me.'

'It's just me and Mum. Don't worry, she secretly like the challenge of raising me alone, especially on nights like this.'

'I understand, it's just me and my Mum at home too,' I tell her and that image of Matka, crying at the kitchen table flashes back to me.

Jack catches my eye and gives me a look, maybe he doesn't like me talking to his new girlfriend, or maybe he's feeling guilty about something.

'Jack told me you lived with both your parents.'

'Yeah. Lived. Papa left.'

They insist on letting me rest, but because Barbie's mum is upstairs sleeping, all they do is turn off the lamp and go and stand in the darkness of the kitchen.

With nothing left to focus on, the bruises and cuts on my body begin to ache. I want to get a better picture of what happened, but I know unless I get Jack on his own there's no way I can admit to a blackout.

They wait until I should be sleeping and then their voices drift out the kitchen.

Barbie: 'What happened?'

Jack: 'We got into a fight. It was nothing really.'

Barbie: 'If you got into a fight, how come you're fine and he looks like dog shite?'

I can't help but smile to myself in the darkness. I'd have though Jack would have come up with something better.

'So he got into a fight and you pulled him out?' she says. There's a pause and I can almost hear Jack's brain trying to think of a better story.

'Come on, that's hardly fair, it wasn't his fault you know.'

'I saw him at the party. All that stuff with Katie, it's not like he isn't fond of trouble.'

'This is totally different, for a start, this wasn't his fault. That stuff with Katie too, that girl is a nutcase you know that.'

A cup thumps onto the table followed by the slosh of its contents. 'You don't even know him.'

'You can clean that up,' Barbie says in mock anger, a cough building up in her throat, 'and you can tell me what happened.'

'Okay, lay off,' Jack says and already I'm thinking that picture of innocence in the living room is just the trick of her body and the real Barbie, the one I've heard so many stories about, is out there in the dark.

'Don't forget you pulled my mum out of bed for this. She'd only been home twenty minutes.'

At first there is only a whisper, a single hushed voice competing with the traffic outside to be lost in my mind and then I can make out Jack's words.

'We got this opportunity to make some money, I can't go into the details, it's not fair on Charlie, but let's just say it got out of hand. It was my fault and he paid the price.'

There's a spark from a match and for a second Jack is illuminated by the joint he is lighting, his face contorted by the words.

'Where did this opportunity come from?'

'I dunno, I didn't know them, they just got my pager number from somewhere. It was weird, but get this, we made a packet.'

'So it worked out alright then?'

'Lucinda, he could have died. I could have been responsible.'

Jack stops talking and I try to feel something, any emotion, but I feel blank so I fill my brain with the crackle of Jack tightly inhaling smoke and wait for the rest of the story.

'Major.' Barbie sighs.

'This is real. You should see my fucking car, it's soaked with blood.'

'Your car, *your car*,' she apes, 'what about our fucking sofa?' she lets out this hysterical laugh that echoes through the house.

My eyes close and when I open them again Jack is wedged in a small space on the end of the sofa, and the curtains have been opened, bathing everything in this soft milky moonlight.

A musty woolen blanket is weighing my body down, comforting the aches beneath it.

'Where's Barbie?' I croak.

'Upstairs, asleep.'

We look at each other and I try and work out how messed up my face is by looking at the expression on his. 'I'm sorry mate, it all got a bit out of hand.'

Jack passes me my money, keeping his eyes on his hands, peeling off notes from a roll as if he's a fat businessman.

He hands me nearly three times the rate I've heard you can charge for a blowjob. At first I think he's giving me his share too because of what happened, but it can't be. This is still too much cash. 'But I got you out in time, right?'

'Your pager, it went off before we met those guys.' I tell Jack. 'This was arranged.'

'So, it was just a deal. Nothing important.'

'From the message Judy left as a joke, in the toilet?' I ask. Jack just shrugs his shoulders. 'I guess,' he mumbles.

Then it hits me and I wonder just how I could have been so fucking stupid.

'They paid to beat me afterward, didn't they?' but I don't even need him to reply to know it's true.

His eyes dart away but there's enough moonlight for me to see his face.

'Get some sleep, yeah? We'll sort it in the morning.'

CHARLIE

Last night I lost my bearings a little, I admit that. Jack and I got tossed in the deep end and when it was sink or swim, I sunk.

I sunk so deep I am still underwater now.

This morning, lying on Barbie's sofa, I know things will be different. Things have to be different because I'm still alive. I'm still here.

Get over it or let it kill you, right?

After all, the sun has risen and I've got my wallet full of cash. Cuts heal. Bruises heal. Scars make a man.

Besides, I've had shit kicked out of me enough times by Papa to know that it always hurts more the next day, but after that you start to get better. So if I can cope with this, I can cope with anything.

Heaving to a sitting position gives me a flash of dizziness, so I lie back down and start with smaller, easier movements. I go to touch my face, but it feels numb. Like a lightning bolt, I remember what felt like a set of knuckles connect with my jaw.

I close my eyes, trying to tune into the memory, hoping more of the picture will come back. At the moment, it's just the feelings, no sounds and no images.

The hand belongs to one of the men from the factory. That much I can guess. The skin on his hand was rough, so rough it felt like he was coated in scales.

I wiggle my toes which all seem to be responding from inside my socks somewhere underneath the blanket.

There's no flashback.

I roll my tongue over my teeth, a thick gunk sticks to the walls of my mouth and makes it hard for me to swallow. Nothing. I don't even want to think about the blood and spit and vomit coating my gums.

It seems like that glimpse of the night before is all my broken memory will give me, then I arch my back. Another twinge from one of them putting their boot across my spine, a half memory of inhaling biscuit dust.

Then it all clicks into place. The scaly punch, it wasn't a fist meeting my jaw, it was my jaw hitting the concrete.

I wait, hoping that the first of my grey-outs to ever return to me will grow and grow until I have the whole picture, in glorious Technicolor playing in my head.

I make an inventory while I wait:

Number of teeth chipped: one.
Number of ribs bruised, or cracked: three.
Number of cuts and bruises visible: five.
Number of stitches needed: unknown at present.
Number of pounds sterling in my wallet: ninety.

My mouth is dry so I chew roughly on nothing, letting my tongue loll around my skull imagining a juicy apple crunching between my jaws and not a dead lump of meat for a tongue, anything to produce a steady trickle of saliva. I swear when I chew my tongue rustles like paper. Slowly my throat warms up enough to give out a loud, alien cry.

I want someone to come and find me, I want Jack to apologise and then fill in the gaps to prod my memory into action.

The noise rattles through the house but the disturbance is so brief, I begin to think I never made the sound at all. I know Barbie's bedroom is at the top of the stairs and even with a mouthful of saliva my voice wouldn't carry that far.

That's when it occurs to me that the house is deadly silent. Somehow, I suddenly know for sure that no one is in. I shift the curtains, not wanting to look. The drive is empty.

If the Ford has gone then Jack has gone. The surge of anger forces me into a sitting position and in my head I am already halfway down the street, calling out his name, ready to avenge the night before. The bastard has left me here.

Hoping for comfort in cash, I reach for my wallet thinking how almost all of my share will have to go on repairing my beautiful hair extensions, which are half torn out and matted with blood and shit.

The familiar brown leather in my palm feels like a secret handshake, the wallet has purified the money overnight.

Or it would have if my wallet weren't empty.

I wait until my thirst and anger overwhelm me, I focus on the emotions, converting them into energy so I can get to the sink or the fridge, anywhere with water.

I hold my breath and the anger to energy change begins to take place, like emotional photosynthesis, like Bruce Banner after a line of coke.

I rush to the breakfast bar, half stumbling, half charging. The dash to the counter is enough to bring on another attack of the dizzies and I'm clutching onto the bar like it's supporting my entire body, which it probably is. For a second I feel an intense moment of paranoia, like this whole episode, the ride with Judy, the men, this morning is all one big test and Papa is in on, like a crazy initiation into adulthood, but it passes as soon as my body takes over, demanding fluids and I start moving toward my goal of cool milk.

As my feet hit the tiles, a disgusting nausea rises up and my thighs start shaking uncontrollably. I make it to the fridge and glug down a pint, and when the liquid hits my mouth, a thousand tiny cuts burst to life and there are so many of them you'd think I spent the night munching on glass.

The lush comfort of the milk reaches my throat and any stings evaporate as I wipe my lips, putting the empty carton back in the fridge. I have to sit at the breakfast bar for a long time.

The dizziness seems linked to a headache – probably from sleeping so long in the cold. I follow the milk with half a chocolate bar and some nuts that are on the side and the sickness drifts in and out until it disappears. In between munching I touch the scratches and mud on my legs, arms and any other easily reachable body parts.

I pat my hair slowly, feeling the braided extensions. One comes out in my hand, that too, has mud on it. When all the nuts have gone I try walking around the kitchen. I still ache but it's possible.

Slowly it dawns on me that the house really is deserted, as is the drive, the Ford has gone.

In the hall is an ashtray, half filled with butts, a glass with an inch of juice left in it and the print of Barbie's thick lipstick around the rim. This is all that's left of them, a few dirty bits of crockery and an even dirtier boy.

I consider looking upstairs, maybe seeing if Barbie's Mum is in to give me a lift home but when I put my foot on the first step it makes a loud creaking noise and my legs hurt so much I actually wince. The sound in the silent house shakes me a little and suddenly I just want to leave. Facts remain, there's no note, no sign of abduction and no Ford outside, so I pick up my tea flask and leaving the front door wide open walk the forty minute journey back to my house.

The Casio reads 0939. I wish I had a better coat, or at least something to hide my dress. The cold is enough to keep my pain away and soon I am thinking back to the night before.

So, Jack gets a page and some man asks, actually has to say the words, to arrange for us to meet him and explain exactly what he and his cuntish friends want to do to me.

What did the person who types out the pager message think? I always wonder about that, how you can score some weed or send a dirty message or, I don't know, ask to beat around a kid after getting him to suck you off, when you have to repeat the message to a stranger and spell any complicated words like fellate?

Where is Jack? You don't just leave your friend alone in a strange house, but then before last night I thought a lot of different things about Jack.

I am so angry I have to stop thinking by counting the steps it takes to reach my home - four thousand, three hundred and thirty seven. Maybe. That's how many it feels like, I lost count a few times. Two and a bit miles.

Back at step twenty five I turned to check that I had left the door open and another ten steps later stopped, while I thought about going back to close it. At the one thousandth mark I got a bit lost as well, it's hard to count out loud in four figures, especially when you can see your breath in front of you.

I wonder if Poland is this cold. Matka says that Poland was harsh to Papa, that Poland made him the he way he is now.

I can't imagine it's that different, unless in Poland it's legal to terrorise your family, which would explain a lot really. I'm pretty sure it's not, but I might look it up the next time I go to the library.

There are enough steps left in the journey for me to work out exactly how I'd pay Jack for letting those men beat me. It starts with simple stuff, a reversal of situations where I am watching him getting hammered by some men, then maybe humiliated by someone he loves and finally paying him a pittance before stealing it back.

Tell his Dad that he's funding the nasty little habit Judy has picked up or about the twelve ounces of grass hidden under the porch of their house.

That isn't enough though, none of it is, not even all those things together. I need something more than just payback. I need to balance things out between us, to make them as they were before so that last night becomes a memory, just another point in our relationship and I just don't know how to do that.

Cut off a limb maybe or even just a finger so every time he's taking a wank he has to think about how he betrayed the one person who would never let him down.

Except now all that has changed. He has broken something between us and in order for us to carry on I've got to do something to set the balance right. I decide that I will wait for him to come to me, to ask forgiveness and then, when the time is right, when the opportunity presents itself I will take it.

The journey between the houses takes me to the edge of our estate, where I can either march right through and risk being savaged by children and dogs or walk the perimeter adding another three hundred footfalls to my journey.

I choose the long way, partly because I look like a victim and partly because I don't want to face anyone yet. My head hurts, my wallet is empty and my heart feels swollen. Where is Jack?

Inside my house I ignore both the calls and the looks of horror on Matka's face when she sees the state I'm in. I walk to the bathroom and start to pull out the ruined extensions.

They look like the tails of dead rodents, most have flecks of blood and mud encrusted in them. Later, I take them out to the back yard and put them in the big bins. That night, I swear I see a local dogs munching on one.

Next, in the kitchen Matka is silently crying as she dabs antiseptic on my head and ribs. I'd like to talk to her, to tell her what I'm doing, how I get in these states but I just don't know where to begin. She looks crumpled, like a balloon that's been deflated.

'Did someone attack you because we're immigrant?' she asks. This kind of question is exactly why I can't talk to her. I want to though. I want to tell her this country is made of immigrants and that it's my dress, not my nationality, that get me in trouble.

I want to tell her how I blank things out, I know I do but I can't stop it.

I want to tell her that there's nothing medically wrong with me as far as I can tell and she can stop reading old medical journals looking for reasons her son has memory blocks and a weakness for dressing like her twenty years ago.

I want to tell her I don't know how things got this bad, that I'm sorry, it looks like I've ruined another Christmas and how sometimes at night I think I will close my eyes and when they open I'll have blanked out her leaving and she'll just be gone.

I don't say any of this to her of course, just hiss when the antiseptic reaches the red scratches on my bony white body.

When she finishes we sit together on the sofa, me in my own male clothes that she dressed me in, her in a cardigan Papa bought her the year I was born. She reaches into her purse, a big embroidered thing and hands me forty pounds all in crushed five pound notes. Exactly enough money to have my extensions refitted.

We sit together cradling mugs of over brewed tea whilst watching the local news. It turns out Barbie's house has been robbed.

When six o'clock passes without a phone call from Jack, Matka gets up and turns the TV off.

She puts her dry, limp hand on mine and says, 'Did you have a fall out with Jack?' and I just sit there, letting her hand rest on mine, not daring to admit what happened in case it makes it true.

I have never argued with Jack before, never walked away from him. There had never been a need to.

We met on the way to a party. His dealer lived in the same road as this guy I knew called Rich, he was just some semi-retarded boy in my school, but he seemed to like me and we got chatting. It wasn't actually Rich's party but his sister's. I was waiting outside the petrol station with some kids in my year, while Rich-the-retard went to buy alcohol.

He was a few years above us in school and easily looked the over eighteen. Somehow his low IQ made it hard for shop assistants to question his age.

Rich always carried around one of those boiled sweet whistles and liked to hang it around his neck at parties so he could make noise and shower people in spit.

It was like he spent his whole life imagining he was at a rave in a field somewhere and not living a suburban kid's life. He was nice, always bringing me food or weed, trying to get me to go to the arcade. I honestly don't think he ever realised I was a boy.

So there I stood waiting for Rich, the cold biting at my flesh, my face red and puffy from squeezing spots that weren't there an hour before. Jack ambled over, his rough brown curls bouncing in his face. My Casio read 20:02 and the sky was flitting somewhere between evening and night, yet he still wore these huge Jackie O glasses, later I found out they were belonged to his mother, the one with the goldfish mouth.

'Hey baby,' he schmoozed in my ear. The heat of his breath against my cold neck felt like swallowing whisky. A pit of fire sparked in my belly.

I pushed my hair behind my ears, this was about a year ago, before I could afford my extensions, I wore a blonde cropped bob.

'You with Rich?' he asked taking off his glasses in one smooth, practiced movement before looking me up and down. Then he paused, his breath caught for a moment.

'Shit, I'm sorry man,' he stumbled, his voice changing more with each word 'You must think I'm a complete prick. You know from over there I thought you were a girl.'

That was it. He'd seen right through me.

That's how I made my closest friend, he gave me some weed he couldn't shift that afternoon at college, and I told him what I was doing in a black cotton dress and fat plastic pearls.

He said he understood. Everyone was into something crazy. He wasn't sure what his thing was. Weed or maybe reggae or porn. They sounded like normal things to me.

He told me maybe if things were different he'd have been giving me my own pearl necklace. That night I went home and actually asked Matka what that meant. Luckily she didn't know either. The next month we got free internet at the library and I never had to ask another question again.

I started hanging around with Jack, just for something to do, just because if I didn't, then I'd be doing nothing.

Less than nothing.

He liked me too. He felt my craziness might compliment the rest of his life.

When I asked what he meant, he told me how his sister Judy had just got back from university, screwed up on a nasty heroin habit and he'd taken to dealing soft drugs at college to pay for rehab. He admitted the irony of the situation. That's what he was doing at the party, meeting Johno at Rich's to pick up some more gear.

'Rich's sister?' Jack shot me a look. I nodded, 'Don't touch her. Filthy. I swear.'

He wiped his palms over his jeans and stuck his long tongue out. It was covered in while felt mush.

'Ok, thanks for the tip.' I nodded again.

'You are into girls, right?'

'Oh yeah course. Girls. I like girls, you know if it has a hole-'

'You fuck it,' he laughed, blowing smoke into the night.

Now I am sitting in my bedroom, in the dark, plotting to punish him and I want to feel like some character out of those black and white samurai films, where the guy stays awake for days, crouched in an alley, waiting to kill his rival for soiling his honour.

Instead I feel like what I am, a pouting greasy kid who is hoping the chance for revenge or reconciliation will just fall in his lap before the clock strikes midnight.

I make, it the chance arrives with a whole eight hours to spare.

It's December 31st, 1997, and the whole world is preparing for another year. At two o'clock this afternoon Matka stops blowing balloons and calls down the basement stairs in a breathy voice that I have a visitor.

Instantly Jack's face appears in my mind, but already I know it's not him. He could have had an accident in the Ford, he could be dead. I don't know where he is, just that I doubt he's heading toward my bedroom right now.

Matka calls again but I don't reply and in a few minutes I hear the clack clack clacking of her plastic sandals against the iron steps. Slightly after them is the soft pad of trainers, too light for Jack's step. She ushers my silent guest into my room and disappears back upstairs.

Barbie takes off her winter coat and thumps down onto my bed. A strong smell of cough syrup wafts up my nostrils and begins to permeate the cramped room.

I can't hide my surprise at her being here, nor at the fact that underneath her heavy woolen coat she is wearing a flimsy peach nightgown.

'Did you hear my house got robbed?' she asks.

'Yeah,' I tell her, 'Did they steal your clothes too?' but before she can answer she has started coughing. First politely, with her hand over her mouth, little girly sound, then harsher until she is standing again, clutching her ribs, one long spasm after another.

Her coat has fallen open and the nightgown is static stuck over the shapes of her body. I'm pretty sure she isn't wearing any underwear.

I watch all of this from the considerable safety of the corner of my bedroom. When she has finally finished she flings her body onto my bed in mock exhaustion.

My eyes follow the hemline of her gown as it rises an inch when she lays back.

It's weird, I know what's coming but this is nothing like that time with Katie, then I felt like some kind of slick prowler, completely in control and with one firm objective.

Now, I just want Barbie to get the hell away from me.

I keep thinking I should ask about Jack, just to find out if he's alive and everything, just to know what the fuck is going on, but I don't, I just can't bring myself to do it, like by asking I've let him win. Pride is such a skurwysyn, just like Papa always said.

I sit down on my bed next to her, she's heavier than me and it means when I sit her weight drags the mattress down and pulls me a little nearer to her.

One of my hands is touching the edge of her coat and the material feels soft resting against my fingers. I keep thinking about what she wants from me, beyond the surface, beyond her skin pressed against mine.

Girls don't often turn up in my room looking all sexy in their night clothes and winter coat, but I'm telling myself there's got to be more to it than that and then it hits me - this is all about Jack.

Why would Jack disappear from my life only to send me the girl he's been messing around with? Is she a trap? A gift? Or an apology? Or, has he gone off the deep end and she's decided to get at him by coming to me.

A samurai makes his decisions in seven breaths.

Whatever the reason she's been driven to me, I've decided this is the way I am going to punish Jack and with it, I get the added promise of kissing my Virginity goodbye.

I'm about to leap on her but that thing that always stops me starts to shake in my belly, like a little creature that wakes up every time I try to get something going with a girl.

It's only mission in life is to make sure I keep my Virginity plastic wrapped in original casing and as soon as it feels a stirring in my jockeys it's up and awake and ready to piss on my lust by pointing out every distraction around and every imperfection a girl has.

So her thighs are too large, verging on heavy, even. It's nothing I can't get over. How bad could it be? I imagine her stretch marks. I bet she was one fat kid. Cramming chocolate bars in her mouth anytime no one was looking.

She's got a good body overall, nice hair, clean nails. I sound like Matka. I try to think of something sexy, something arousing. That's a good word, arousing. Even the word sounds hot. Better than *seksowny*.

I think of Barbie alone at home getting ready to see me, trying on different outfits. Kissing another girl, maybe a blonde. I think of her in a big bath full of clear, hot water, calling me in, just waiting to crush my Virginity between her meaty thighs.

'You want to see it?' she asks, propping herself up on one elbow.

'Sorry? What do you mean?' but I know what she means, it's her opening line, it's her one trick, her calling card. It's the one thing, or two things, that make her unique.

I wonder if that offer roles off her tongue at every party she goes to, every guy she's met. I don't care though, because now I am one of those guys. A soon to be member of the double-hole club.

She smiles, looks down her own body, patting lightly where her knickers should start but don't.

I've seen girls naked, but I've never one with two anuses.

Now I know we're going to do it, it's not enough to just go for it. I want to hear her say it to me.
'No Barbie, I don't want to see your extra hole. You're with Jack.'

She kicks off her trainers and I hold my breath, waiting for the magic words that will make my vengeance complete.

'I don't want Jack, I want you.'
Bingo.

What a bastard I am. This is the last December 31st I will be young, free and innocent and I am spending it fucking my best friend's girlfriend, wait for it, in the vagina. I'm taking a trip down the birth canal.

I thought I'd be hammering out my Virginity by getting to guest in her famous rear, but she says she wants to lose it, her own Virginity that is, and her vaginal Virginity at that.

She says to me all coy, whether it's true or not I don't know, but she says to me although many boys and a few men have taken her up both her anuses, none have yet to steal her true Virginity. Just not interested.

Would you believe it? I am the one she wants to give it to.

I should be like winning an Oscar but somehow I feel like I've got the consolation prize.

She doesn't even ask about my V status so I just shut up and plough on.

Having sex isn't that different from all the other stuff before it really, except that it requires a lot more energy on the man's part.

In some ways I actually think a blowjob might be better, but this is my first time and I'm willing to give it a chance to see if it grows on me. Still, I'm actually having sex, like right now, my Virginity is working its way out of me like a tapeworm wrapped around a pencil and somehow I've managed to complete this achievement just hours before my fifteenth birthday.

But boy, vengeance is hard work, and Barbie seemed like the romantic type to start with, lots of stroking and kissing and saying little things in my ear, which was cute at first but now it turns out she can't shut up, which would be okay except for what she's saying.

While we're doing it, she tells me in no uncertain terms that she can't let Jack have her the way the good Lord intended because she first needs to fuck someone who isn't her boyfriend and isn't ugly.

'Jack isn't ugly, he's one of the most attractive people I know.' I'm calling my best friend attractive while my penis is inside his girlfriend.

Too weird.

'Basically, I don't want him in my memory for the rest of my life.' She tells me, while I am on top of her, my skinny hip bones pushing into the soft wads of flesh above her thighs.

It's hard work and she's lying there as if at a beauty parlour chatting away, rolling her eyes back and gesturing with her hands. Why didn't I just have sex with Katie? That could have got pretty hot while it was going on, couldn't it? Even if it was a trick.

'I just need to get this first time out of the way, then it'll be fine.' Barbie says.

Her tone is idle and uninterested, she must be trying to stop me from coming, her chosen method of contraception: insult and boredom.

My butt aches, my thighs ache. My ribs sting when I breathe.

I grab her hands and wedge them tight underneath the weight of her lower back, pressing all nine stone of me against her, listening as her breath grows more shallow as her lung capacity diminishes.

She seems to like it, but I don't feel anything special. The only good bit is when she has a coughing fit and all the muscles in her vagina tighten in a spasm, and it's like there's a tiny WWF team working on my cock but the fit is over as quickly as it started.

I just want to finish now.

Who the fuck loses their Virginity as a vengeance against their best friend anyway?

I go through a series of scenarios to try and reach a climax, but my brain just punishes me. I jump to Matka listening at the top of the stairs or Jack coming in, his face on seeing us together.

I imagine I am killing Barbie, that slowly if she doesn't wear me down through boredom, I can persevere and fuck her to death. After a while my thoughts lazily drift back to Katie on the lawn, I create a new ending to our last meeting, her muted squeals dying out completely as Papa's hammer slams against her pretty skull, which scares me.

It's as if these images surface from the murky, most masculine part of me, then they just kind of take over.

I force myself into focus and Barbie is still underneath me, now with her eyes closed and her head rolled back so I can see the fat around her chin, like a sleeping pug dog.

In the end I just force it out by thinking of the filthiest porn I can remember, some Latino woman sucking a horse and then another one where a bunch of guys are showering this girl in a foreign hotel room, pretty routine stuff.

I don't quite know what to do next to indicate I'm done so I just kind of lay still on her until she pulls her hands out from under her and I climb off, I do all of this without even bothering to make an orgasm noise.

As soon as I'm done with Barbie, all the weird thoughts drift back around my head, until that sleepy safe feeling after climax clears away all things nasty and all things wrong.

I stare at her trainers lying in the middle of my floor and marvel at them like they are evidence in executing my revenge, because now I know, whatever has happened to Jack, whether he knows it or not right now, we are even.

Her trainers are Adidas, a popular choice at my school. They look tiny, maybe a size four. I think about telling her Adidas produce international kits for most football teams, including Poland. She probably already knows.

Barbie gets up and uses both her hands to straighten her thick black hair as if it were a wig, then begins to look into a small mirror to fix her make-up. I force myself to hold my breath and count to thirty before I ask about Jack. I make it to twelve.

'Have you seen Jack then?' I ask as casually as I can. Probably not the best opener after you've just had sex with someone, but I need to know. Barbie flips the mirror down and looks at me.

'What do you think?'

'And that's why you're here? To get him back for running off?'

'I'm here because I want to be. I don't mind that you're a bit weird, or that you're German.'

'I'm Polish,' I say.

'Same difference.'

'Tell that to the Polish. You need to use Encarta. Seriously, it has everything in there. Do you know Saint Bernards hyper-salivate because of a genetic defect?'

'What the fuck, Charlie?'

I wait, one thing I've learned about girls is that if they don't want to talk about something, they rely on you to steer the conversation to something else. If you shut up, they'll tell you more, it's like they can't help it, they're programmed that way.

'We had a fight,' she waits to make sure I am listening, 'about you, actually.' I try a solemn nod and it's enough to get her talking, 'I mean, don't flatter yourself or anything, it was more about what you did and the money. That's all.

'He was feeling bad about, well you know what, and he shouted at me so I made him leave. I haven't seen him since that night, you know, the night before we were robbed.' Barbie finishes off her make-up and snaps the mirror tightly shut. 'Anyway, it doesn't matter now. I don't think I'll be seeing him around after this.'

I feel sick. All the post sex chemicals that were keeping me safe and sleepy detach themselves and leave though the pores of my skin and I realise I've made a huge mistake.

Jack didn't desert me. Barbie made him leave when he put me first, yes, that's what happened.

I wasn't having vengeance sex, she was.

There's still time to recover, they've only been together for a week and if she's right, they're not going to see each other again.

All I need to do is get rid of the evidence. Then I can find Jack and re-grow my Virginity. Maybe if I have sex with someone else today it won't count.

I'm sitting on my bed, staring at the creases in my sheets, knowing I can't tell anyone how I lost my Virginity and wondering how I can stop the last half hour replaying in my head.

If Barbie was telling me the truth about her arguing with Jack then I've just made the biggest mistake of my life so far.

I should call Jack and straighten things out, find out for myself what happened. I keep thinking I'll go upstairs and just call him, but I stay staring at rumples in the sheets, thinking how they were made by Barbie's wide arse.

I never did get to see her mystery hole.

She's evidence now and she needs to stay out of our lives. Maybe we'll see her at a party or something but she'll just look over at us and then keep chatting to whoever she's trying to pull. I'm already imagining my life back on track.

Everything is going to be fine.

But for some reason I feel very alone, it's not that I miss Barbie, obviously, it's more that I feel like I've lost something, like I've been yanked from one place to another far too quickly. Maybe this is what girls feel like after a one night stand.

Barbie has left her little mirror and I open it and stare at my face. It doesn't look any different. I pull a grimace and then a big wide grin.

My teeth look yellow and when I think about it, I can't remember the last time I cleaned them.

I wonder if when I see Jack next, he'll be able to tell what's happened and if he asks me directly, if I'll be able to lie about it.

A tightness keeps clutching my chest, like my ribcage is shrink wrapping around my heart. It seems revenge is pretty nasty, especially as it looks like it was uncalled for on my part.

I suppose I could have gone with my plan B and asked his mum, the goldfish, for a blowjob, but I think everyone involved would have ended up feeling embarrassed.

I figure I'll call Jack now, get things fixed, but Matka is on the phone. I stand over her, watching her fingers curl and uncurl around the cord. When I don't leave she turns to face the other way.

I walk across the common and onto the estate, running my fingers over the rough concrete walls, listening to my shoes scuff the pavement in time with my heartbeat.

It's getting dark and the kids on the estate are moving together in little packs of threes or fours looking for that post-Christmas fight.

The estate hasn't seen any violence on the streets for days and you can feel it building up, the tension ready to break free, become a presence of its own.

Going deeper into the estate is something I don't normally do. It's like stepping back in time, the cars that are left on the street were all made before I was born and it seems like one in ten of them have been broken into, glass littering the streets like a sparkling sea.

I walk randomly up and down paths, killing time until I can get hold of Jack, taking turns on a whim. I find a street I like the sound of and take it, then do the same with the next and then next, until I've lost my sense of direction. First Worthing Road, then Fawcett, then Allen's Road. Allen's Road has been carefully graffiti'd to read *Alien's Road*.

I look in the windows of the people that live in Aliens Road and wonder how many of them are Virgins. Number 12 has a ginger cat lazing in the window, possibly a Virgin.

Number 17, two old people dancing together in what looks like a bare room - unlikely Virgins. Number 39 is different enough to make me stop. It has an old bottle green door which is normal enough, but the door is open.

Inside the hallway is so yellow, I feel warmer just by looking at it. What if I go in, pretend to be an orphan, would they adopt me? I could walk inside, turn left at the end of the hall and find myself sitting at a pine table, my place already laid for dinner, the only reason to get up would be to wash my hands before I eat.

The woman would turn around, holding this huge plate of food and she'd look at me and smile. Except the woman isn't Matka so I can't go in. Matka is sitting alone in our kitchen, holding up the phone.

A plastic holly wreath has fallen from the front door and is lying on the concrete path. I step nearer, reaching out to touch it but an ambulance pulls up to the house and two young paramedics rush in and moments later come back with a young man fading in and out of consciousness.

Everything seems to be moving in double time.

Between the glow of the hall and the reflective uniforms of the paramedics the man looks like an angel.

His hair is blonde like mine, but natural in colour. I bet he's not a Virgin.

He is lifted into the back of the ambulance and several girls pile in after him, eagerly waiting for a response from the angel.

His hair has fallen into his face and he leans against one of the girls for support. The paramedics push them back – the angel needs air to breathe.

Someone says the word *overdose* and I wonder what happened to the angel to get him so down, to make him so ill.

Then the doors close and the ambulance pulls away, and as I watch it go the streetlights blink to life. I realise I am holding my breath.

By the time I find my way home, downstairs is empty and dark. Two plates rest in the sink, along with a mug and a Tupperware box covered in grime. There are red balloons everywhere, you can't walk without kicking one. Matka is upstairs, probably napping, so I can't ask if Jack has called. I put my hand on the telephone and think about calling him, but its New Year's Eve, he'll probably be out already. I walk past the phone and down the stairs leading to my bedroom.

I'm lying on my bed in a state of fever, my feet are pressed up against the cool of the concrete wall, and my head is tucked between my knees, like they might stop the thoughts rumbling through my head.

I'm like this, creased and folded closed when my window creaks open and the agile body of my best friend slips though.

Jack stands in the bedroom and everything looks new. The whole afternoon slips away and by the time he smiles I have erased the last few days.

He doesn't say sorry exactly, but he does give me back the money from my wallet, explaining that he needed to borrow it to get away for a bit to clear his head and that he'd just got back.

'Have you seen anyone else yet, since you've got back?' I ask, making sure to keep things vague. But he's only seen Judy.

Jack says he's been camping in a wooded area just out of town, I guess that means he's been sleeping in the Ford and getting stoned.

He says he wanted to take Judy with him, but that their parents have finally put her in a recovery program and she has to check into the hospital every morning for counselling and methadone.

'I just needed to work out what happened and why, you know at the factory.' He's not looking at me but I nod anyway. 'It won't happen again, Charlie.'

We sit on the bed and he rolls a joint, I faintly find myself worrying about Matka smelling it, but she's several floors above us, probably resting.

'What's new with you?' Jack asks, and I wish I'd changed the sheets.

There are two hours until the New Year begins and when the clock strikes midnight people everywhere will be thinking about themselves and who they are kissing, if they are lucky enough to be kissing anyone at all. I will be turning fifteen.

Jack wants me to go with him to break into a house, steal everything we can carry and then trash the place.

Of course, I agree.

For it to work, well, for us not to get caught, we have to get into the house at eleven thirty and leave by midnight. This is the time most people are out of their houses, because they're at parties, major landmarks like the pier, or just out on the streets.

While they're out celebrating the beginning of a New Year, commenting to each other how wonderful it is that people, strangers even, can get along so peacefully we'll be in their houses stealing their week old Christmas presents then fucking up their perfect carpets.

Jack has it all worked out and he tells me by pulling this off he's going to make it up to me, for all that other stuff that went bad. I don't look at him when he says this, but I'm sure if we get out of my bedroom he won't sense that I've already taken my payback for the night in the car park without his permission.

'Just see it like a game, a game of Smash and Grab, we'll have a laugh, nothing heavy.'

Jack heads up the stairs and I check my face in the reflection of my window, then the sheets, then my face again, looking for signs of betrayal, signs of a girl.

I push the little bedroom window wide open, air out the last wisps of Barbie.

In the living room, we wade through bright red balloons, knee deep and squeaking for attention. To please Matka, Jack and I make a fuss, batting the balloons around until one pops, and suddenly it seems like we can't stop stamping on the little rubber ovals, bursting them with our heavy feet and savouring the sound.

Jack guides Matka to the sofa, chatting, cheery, flashing his straight white teeth that match his clear skin until she relaxes and begins to talk to him.

I sneak into the dark kitchen and start to search as quietly as I can for anything that looks like it could cause some damage. It's hard in the dark and I feel around beneath the kitchen sink, trying not to jerk away every time I touch a wet patch or furry old cloth.

I can hear Matka talking to Jack about her childhood in Europe, about one New Year when she saw a synagogue get burned to the ground. Through all of this I bet Jack is smiling, a polite nod here, a small twitch there, like he understands everything she's ever seen. When I walk back into the room with a can of spray paint that was bought for my bike, he's got her tiny hands in his and she doesn't even look up at me.

She never talks about any of this to me, even though she sometimes accuses me of not listening, that's not what it is.

She doesn't think I'm ready for it, to hear about her life before me. She doesn't think I'm ready for it and she doesn't think I can do anything about it.

Because Jack is bigger than me, steadier, she can tell him about the things in her past that still hurt or amaze her, because he would understand, he might actually do something about it. Not like her son, who comes home in cuts, bruises and women's clothes.

I slip the spray paint in Jack's bag and head back to the kitchen. I find a half used bottle of bleach, a tin of pink gloss that we used for the toilet room in the basement. I wait for the conversation to start up again but it seems to have run dry.

I wonder what they could be doing in the silence and then the image of them kissing flashes in my head and I move quickly but quietly back into the living room. But they're just sitting there, Matka staring into nothing and Jack waiting for her to come back to life. She looks like some wind-up doll that's run its motor out. I dump the items in Jack's bag and cough when neither of them notice I'm back in the room.

Matka turns to face me, Jack's hands still clasping hers. With the kitchen light off, it's the single bulb in the living room glowing above them that makes me see a yellowy bruise resting on her cheek.

The colour taunts, it is old, maybe even a week. Why haven't I noticed? Before I can ask anything Jack cuts in.

'Where'd you get the bruiser Mrs. L?' Matka shies away coyly as if he'd asked her out on a date.

'Oh you know how it is Jack, accidents happen,' She nods the cryptic answer and continues like a toy dog until the three of us are bobbing our heads in silent unison, and because we all seem to be nodding, it looks like we've accepted her answer.

Could it have been Papa? Has he been here? I want to ask but there is no time, I've got a robbery to get to. I am in a western now, the world is black and white and I can hear the film running, feel an audience waiting for my performance. I can't let them down, can't get sucked in here.

Sometimes, more when I was younger I'd picture Matka at my age. I imagined her fiercely protective of her faith, imaginative and artistic.

And beautiful, so beautiful, that even someone made-up couldn't measure up to her.

Slowly it seemed that young girl disappeared and hid deep inside the cracked adult woman, the mother that kissed me goodnight. I wondered if that girl would ever come back. I'm still wondering.

Exchanging the usual jokes of *see you next year* we walk through the shreds of balloons and are out of the door.

As I climb in the Ford, I see Matka clutching the living room drapes, and she watches us until the car glides out of view.

It's New Year's Eve 1997, an hour before my birthday and Jack and I are on our way to play Smash and Grab in one of the neighbouring areas.

He slips a small bottle of whisky out of his coat pocket and we take turns downing the sour amber liquid. I'm waiting to feel the buzz, hear the music that I need to hear so we can play this new game, but the drink isn't touching me in the way I want it to.

The first hit stings my lips, where they are still split and bruised from the night in the car park and now instead of relaxing me I begin to feel a light panic fizz in my stomach, like Jack may be leading me into something awful again.

He nudges me to pass him the bottle and I do, hoping secretly that maybe a Police car will speed by and catch him with it in his hand, then we won't have to go through with the break in.

Nothing like that happens, Jack takes a long glug, and I watch a big wobbly air bubble rise to the surface of the whisky before he takes the bottle away from his mouth. It seems to take forever and I wonder how people can watch the road when they drive while they're tilting their heads back to drink.

I guess Jack is a pretty good driver.

We park in a road with big detached houses running along both sides. Across from the Ford one of these houses is having a party and kids, not much younger than us spill out onto the lawn and the pavement.

I decide that 1998 will be a year of calm for me, no more getting money in stupid, painful and illegal ways, I only ever spend it on girl's clothes and grass anyway. Soon I'll be back to school and maybe then I can start to hang around with some normal kids, like that girl that helps me with my maths problems or some of the guys in my science group.

While I'm looking out the window, deciding that this break in will be the last dumb thing I do for money, Jack is fiddling around with a tin box from his coat pocket. He asks me to block the window, so I unclip my seatbelt and move positions, so my back is against the glass on my side of the car.

Jack measures out a line of fine white powder on the dashboard and, through a ten pound note begins to shuffle the powder up his nose.

He draws another line and this time hands me the rolled up note.

I look at it, the flash of orange and a tiny bit of the Queen's face, not her nose but just an eye and the corner of her mouth, so it looks like she might be smiling.

I shake my head and Jack shrugs, repeating the process himself. There's loads of it left, in the imprints of the plastic dashboard and even a tiny bit on the edge of the steering wheel. Jack's bends down and lets his thick felt tongue wipe up any traces of the drug.

We get out of the car and Jack insists we don't bother to lock it because luck is on our side. I shrug, but he doesn't see because he's already walking down the street, and I rush to catch up with him, fall in step and try to let his courage seep into me.

The roads are in neat grids and soon I've lost which way we'd need to go to get back to the Ford, but it doesn't matter because Jack is leading the way and he says he's sure of where he is going.

The house Jack picks looks like all the others in the street. A green square lawn, bushes on either side, some huge fucking footlights I plan not to set off.

The difference between this house and most of the others my coked up accomplice reminds me is that this house has no lights on. The rich family are out giving us a chance to get what we want.

I stand cold and slightly drunk, rubbing my arms while Jack fiddles with the front door trying to prize open the lock. When I mumble to Jack that I'm cold and maybe we should just forget about the break in, he slips off his coat and hands it to me. It's too big, but it's warm and it has a sour smell that belongs to Jack.

After days of not seeing him, it's kind of comforting in a weird way.

I am looking down at the white outline of my trainers fuzz in and out of focus with the concrete floor when Jack finally gets the door open. We both rush in and it's loud and clumsy but I don't care, we're just savouring the stale warmth inside.

The house is really dark and it just gets worse when we close the front door behind us. Jack rushes blindly upstairs and I waste what seems like minutes just standing in the hall, letting my eyes grow accustomed to the lack of light.

It's just too much like a dream, being in this big empty house and while Jack dashes about upstairs I wander from room to room touching bits of furniture, letting the textures rub against my hands, wondering if this is what life is like for blind people, without the fear of being discovered, of course.

From upstairs Jack shouts that we have fifteen minutes until midnight, the time when we should get out of the house by.

I'm still in the hall, so I look around there for something to steal. By now my eyes are letting me identify objects in the dark. I pick up a camera and slide it into my satchel, on the stairs is a beauty set still wrapped in plastic and I place that carefully on top of the leather camera case.

In the kitchen, I open the fridge and that warm familiar yellow glow bathes three shelves of amazing food. In the centre is the skeletal corpse of a massive turkey, like a ritual sacrifice to the Gods of home refrigeration. I reach out and rub the backbone, its cold and slick.

I put my finger in my mouth and taste the turkey grease. It's good.

The bottom shelf has jar after jar of unknown foods, all without labels. They float aimlessless in thick oils, yellows and browns and reds. I reach for the nearest jar, unscrew it and dip my finger inside. The oil clings to my skin and I hook out a small black oval and put it in my mouth.

It's meaty almost and flakes apart in my mouth. It tastes the way the dirt on common smells after it rains. Like I'm eating a shiny ball of earth. At first I think maybe it's some kind of egg, like the egg of a really small bird, but in the centre is something hard, like a fucking stone.

I spit it out, all wrinkled and rough in my palm. It goes back in the jar.

There's an open glass bottle in the door of the fridge and I glug from it to take away the oily earth taste, but the drink is even worse than the little egg, like I'm drinking medicated toothpaste. I look at the label, ver-mouth. So I was right. Who keeps mouthwash in a glass bottle in their fridge?

There's a bigger room, which I move towards. A bottle of wine rests on a corner table. I think about opening it now, congratulating myself on almost reaching fifteen. Who knows what it will taste like in this backward house?

I'm staring at the bottle when the gold foil seal glows brightly, it's being lit by the headlights of a car driving by outside. I look up just in time to see the room as it would be in the daytime and those few seconds are enough to trigger a little jolt in my memory.

This house looks familiar or feels familiar, like the way a house you've seen before on TV does. There's a memory but maybe it's not your own. But I don't come to this part of town, so I have to presume I'm wrong and the whisky in my stomach encourages me not to think about it and I have to agree that it's more important to get on with the job and get out. I dump the bag in the middle of the living room.

I just need to rest for a minute.

A thud from upstairs, like a piece of furniture breaking, or an angry man, or Jack trashing the place, pulls me away from my thoughts.

I call into the darkness of the house, but there is no reply. Still dizzy, I make my way toward the sound and end up wavering on the bottom step of a huge staircase to call again to Jack. This time he replies, says he's nearly done and I hear a rattle followed by the soft hiss of spray paint projecting from a little can.

I wait, too drunk to care about lifting anything else from the house, just wanting Jack to come downstairs so we can go.

The hall is filled with certificates for some kind of sport, or maybe a martial art, the borders of each framed credential a different bright colour.

The words around the name start to swim and it dawns on me I am going to be sick. I start looking for a toilet. A door to the right leads me into a laundry room. It's too late, this will have to do. I bend over, reach out to balance and while pushing my hands in the dirty silky sheets my throat begins to contract until I feel that all too familiar wave of relief. At the same time a cheer comes from outside as if a crowd of people are congratulating me for relieving my body of alcohol. It's only when I hear a clock chime somewhere within the walls of the house I realise it is midnight.

Its New Year 1998, today is my fifteenth birthday, and I am emptying my stomach into a stranger's laundry basket. My arms buckling, my hands pushing further into the wads of material until by chance they touch something solid. I grip onto it as I wait for the next spasm, steadying myself against the cool, metallic object.
My sweaty palm slides neatly around it until my brain forms the image of a gun. It's enough to make me puke again.

I pull the gun out and look at it. There's a bit of sick on the barrel and I try to wipe it with my sleeve but it just ends up spreading. I don't know much about the gun, it's the first one I've ever held.

I know it's black and it's a handgun. That's all I know about it. I know it's a handgun because the law changed this year to say that you couldn't own one anymore.

I saw a picture of a gun just like this one on the news after a crazy man shot some kids in a school. There was just the one news report. It was only the north. And obviously, I can see the gun is black. I don't know how to open it to see if it's loaded.

The gun and I make our way back into the hall where we find a trail of pink paint that I recognise as the same shade as our bathroom. I follow the steady spats of paint to the lounge, where there is a great big puddle of gloss. In the middle of the puddle is Jack.

We stand in the unlit room facing each other, me with a gun and him looking like he's bleeding paint.

'Let's see,' he calls to me, his arm outstretched, open palm waiting to receive the treasure I have found.

I pass him the gun, cool and solid, coated in a thin layer of vomit. The moment the gun leaves my hand I am sure that something is wrong, that I've made a mistake.

He weighs the gun in his open palm, like you see criminals do in Police shows. 'Feels loaded,' he announces. I look at him, but he's miles away from me, I don't even think he's in this room. Then Jack's grin spreads across his face and I try to read what it means.

I watch Jack's fingers wrap around the gun, his arm lifts, and he turns, grinding the paint into the carpet with his trainers until he's facing me, gun pointed at my head.

And I am thinking I deserve this. Matka is right, I am my own worst enemy.

Jack must know I had sex with Barbie, he must have known all evening. That is the only answer that explains what he is doing right now.

The worst thing is my revenge was futile, Jack didn't abandon me, he left because of guilt and perhaps this is the saddest thing of all, beyond dying, beyond making my fifteenth birthday by an hour only to be shot.

I want my Virginity back.

He's not saying anything, just holding the gun toward me, his teeth so white it's like they're glowing in the dark. I am beginning to think that revenge is like a rubber ball and it just bounces from person to person, making things worse. Only a miracle can save us now.

At some point I drop to my knees, hitting the plush carpet which registers in my brain even at this moment. In my next life I would like to have a bedroom with carpet like this.

Where is that miracle?

If there were a case for divine intervention it would come in the form of a silver Lexus ES 300 pulling into the drive. Time seems to speed up and Jack is tossing the gun to me as if he could catch an STD from it.

Is he scared of being caught with it or scared of using it? The fear seems like fiction already.

As the car crunches over the gravel toward the double door garage it hits a sensor and the lawn lights up, flooding the living room and suddenly everything is in colour, including us.

Jack heads toward the kitchen, looking for a back door. I am frozen by the floodlights blinding me, as if my body will not move until my brain works, it's so bright, like God Himself heard my prayer moments before.

Then my brain connects and I can see the room with the curtains drawn, teenagers cramped into every space, feel the thump of music beneath my feet. That blinding light from the lawn.

This is Katie and Michael's house.

Jack returns to drag me through the house and across a back lawn. There are pink footprints all over the floor, including the ones that mark our escape route. He vaults

89

over the fence in one easy movement and I scrabble quickly after him. I fling myself blindly into the neighbour's garden and end up landing on Jack, bringing him crashing onto the concrete floor.

There's a crunch as I fall onto him and we wrestle. I can feel his body heat against my own, his sour breath in my face, his heavy hands on my back.

He pins me to the concrete easily, but I keep squirming. The gun is in my coat pocket and twice I imagine it going off and maiming one of us. Then Jack lifts an arm and slaps me across the face. It stings but I shut up and keep still.

He lets me up slowly and begins to walk around the garden, wiping off the pink paint from his shoes on a small area of grass.

Behind us are another row of gardens, to the left, Katie's house soon to be filled with angry people. Two gardens to the right a heavy bass and flashing lights indicate a party.

The garden has a dozen people, who from the sound of it are mostly kissing or spaced out, all too wrapped up in starting the New Year to notice two more people entering the party via a backyard fence.

We make our way over, the adrenaline in my body is pumping so hard it makes my calves ache and I am tempted to punch Jack just to let some of the cramp out, uncoil myself. This isn't over, but for now we both have to get out of here.

Jack helps me over both fences and we walk through the party garden. Despite being coked up and covered in paint Jack adopts a relaxed and heavy swagger, he even makes eye contact with a woman, nodding as he pulls back the heavy glass doors and walks into the house.

He saunters across the kitchen and through the hall, the crowd seems older now and we get a few odd looks from strangers, any one of them potentially the owner of the house.

It doesn't matter because we've found the front door and now we're on the tarmac of the street, heading toward the blue Ford, toward home and the future of Jack and I beating each other to death over a girl and a gun.

FOXTROT

It's 0602 but the lights are on when I get home so I skip round to the back and slip in my bedroom window. Legs first I lower myself down, tentatively tapping my foot against my bedroom wall, feeling out for the table to stand on.

Again I wonder if this is what it must be like to be blind. Just as my tendons start to cramp the toe of my trainer reaches the table.

I steady myself, resting my weight for a second only to lose balance and feel the table knocked out from beneath me. I am left hanging, although it's only my arms being tested not my neck.

My face is against the concrete wall and I can smell the damp. If I tasted it I am sure it'd be salty, like human sweat. Seconds pass and the stretching in my triceps turns to a dull ache, then a burning pain and I feel like I've been hanging onto the window ledge of my basement bedroom for an eternity. I could just drop but the noise would bring

Matka downstairs and I can't fall without making a racket. It's then that a pair of arms forms out of the darkness of my bedroom and grab the back of my legs. My hands automatically release their grip and knees bending I am sitting on the shoulders of the person who has lifted me down.

'Matka?' I say instinctively although I know it isn't her, she's not this strong, not this crazy to be lurking in my bedroom with the lights off just before dawn. A strong laugh shudders through my carrier's body and echoes through my own. I almost smile, who else would it be?

'Happy Birthday, son.' Papa places me down beside him, resting a hot hand on my back. I fight the impulse to shake it off and smile up at him. In the darkness I can't make out his features, only his white teeth bared in the moonlight. Its only luck that the gun from Katie's house is safe in my bag and not in my hand.

There's a box on my bed, thin grey cardboard like the boxes from his factory. Papa gestures for me to open it. Inside is a shiny metal instrument. One end has an electrical cable the other a little set of teeth. I pick it up and it feels cold, heavier than I expected. It looks like the kind of thing you'd shear a sheep with. I want to show my appreciation, maybe even use it, but I've no idea why he's given it to me.

Lying at the bottom of the box is a fifty pound note and with the shears in my right hand I go to pick up the note with the other, but Papa stops me, his hand wrapped around my wrist.

He shakes his head slowly and I realise I am going to have to earn the money, my mind flickers through the options before me, what he wants me to do, then it hits me, the way you pick up a smell in a room, suddenly it's there and you know it's been there all along you just weren't in the right place to reach it.

'No, no way,' I tell him, doing my best to look into where I think his eyes should be in the darkness. But the shearers - *clippers* they're called - are out of my hand and Papa is searching for a plug. He keeps his grip on my wrist and reaches blindly behind him, knocking over perfumes and makeup and hair clips until he finds a socket.

I imagine Matka being woken by the noise, sitting bolt upright in bed, straining to hear, maybe even closing her eyes in the darkness to concentrate on the noise.

I'm on my knees and the sound of my bones crashing into the concrete floor rings in my ears long after the pain stops throbbing.

Next Birthday I am asking for a plush rug, a square of that carpet at Katie's. Why the fuck am I always on my knees?

An electrical buzz starts next to my right ear, like a giant wasp, and Papa moves my skull beneath the clippers.

My hair snags on the little blades but soon gives up resistance and I feel the scratchy braids brush my skin as they fall to the floor.

When Papa is finished he turns the box upside down and the note falls on the bed. I keep still until I hear him walk through the kitchen and open the back door.

The sun creeps slowly across my bedroom floor and I watch the light catch my hair, when it was attached to my head I'd never noticed how beautiful it looked. Now, it shines like a pedigree dog.

It's New Year's Day, 1998, my birthday, and all the shops are shut so there's nowhere I can buy a wig.

I try telling myself that there are people who feel worse than me this morning:

Jack – he'll be on a massive downer, probably still asleep on Barbie's lawn.

Barbie, she's a fucked up bitch, even being her must be a major downer.

94

Matka – before the thought can finish I am up the stair in the kitchen. She is standing at the oven, apron on, frying something.

Quality family time – the whole works.

'Happy Birthday, Charlie,' she smiles and I think her face may crack.

She's frying toast and beside the pan there is a plate with at least half a loaf of mighty white already cooked and gone cold. I step closer to her and in the bin there's another ten slices of fried toast.

'Matka, how long have you been cooking me breakfast?' but she doesn't say anything, not about breakfast or about the fact that overnight her cross dressing son has opted for a military haircut.

I try a different technique: 'Notice anything different about me?' I spin on the spot, giving her lots of time to get an eyeful, let her know she'd got time to think about it just in case she's not sure what has changed.

I want to shout at her, ask her who she thinks did this to her child?

'You've had a haircut,' she says, devoid of emotion. I want to throttle her.

The newest fried toast goes on a plate on the table and the pile of cold toast on the side joins its comrades in the bin. She's been up for hours making this for me.

I sit down and eat, almost choking as I try to swallow, wondering why I always mean to be good toward her and end up being a bastard.

Perhaps it's because she is always so unemotional, so numb.

She stands by the oven, clutching the side while I eat and when I've finished she reaches for a box.

I can't help thinking this one may contain some instrument to cut my balls off.

Another party and this time it's my own. Our tiny house is crammed with kids, on the stairs, in the kitchen, in my room, they're everywhere, overtaking the house like some pubescent army.

I recognise most of them from school or from the usual parties I go to. I keep looking out for Barbie, I wouldn't put it past her to show up and tell Jack about our afternoon together.

I'm so paranoid I keep sweeping through the rooms, searching for that jet black hair and the sound of her coughing.

It's eleven and Matka left an hour ago, agreeing to disappear on the condition that the party would be over before 4am.

I agree happily, knowing that by that time I won't care what's going on either way. I'm wearing a white PVC dress because I think it will draw attention away from my now shaven head.

Maybe people with think it's a Tank Girl thing.

I always wonder who picks the music at parties and this one is no different, I don't know who's controlling the stereo and I don't recognise a single track.

It's only eleven o'clock and my head feels muzzled, my brain tightly strapped into place, too large for the skull that contains it. I'm just waiting for Jack to arrive, everything will be fine when he gets here.

I'm working out how to approach a group of girls who are in the year above me at school when Jack steps into the house, pulling Barbie behind him.

He's still got the same paint marked jeans on but his manic smile has gone, replaced with two brown rings around his eyes.

When they approach I smile, hoping neither of them will point out my new look.

It's clear from his face that she still hasn't told him and I'd guess she feels she's got her revenge and is happy to go back to screwing Jack. Of all the things I expected to happen tonight, seeing Jack and Barbie arrive together all smiles was not one of them.

Eventually, Barbie leans in and plants a creamy kiss on my cheek, leaving behind a smudge of purple lipstick. I can smell the cough medicine in the back of her throat and memories of our bodies stuck together push through to the front of my mind and I'm worried my reaction will give us both away.

That doesn't happen, but Jack can sense something is up, I'm sure of it. There's a moment when the three of us freeze, caught in an uncomfortable position: The best friend, his girlfriend and the time you fucked her. If only he knew the whole story.

But it's Jack who breaks the tension, mimicking Barbie's action he lightly kisses my other cheek, then with the cuff of his sleeve wipes the lipstick from my face.

Jack is wearing a green shirt, the kind you see on service people and I wonder vaguely where he got it. My arms reach out to his waist and I hold him close to me so I can look over his shoulder and get an eyeful of Barbie's expression, as if I can tell from one look what she is playing at.

She keeps her eyes down, and I guess she wants things to remain as they are for the moment too. I'm pretty sure if she's being loved by someone, she's content.

The hug turns out to be a memory I want to keep, and I do, long after other details of him fade. For now, Jack laughs and shrugs me off him.

'Hey dude, not so tight, it's not like I am gonna die or something.'

He's wrong of course, within a few weeks he'll be dead. You should never tell someone you're not going to die, face it, it's just stupid.

So I fend off the dumb insults about my lack of hair and move from tiny room to tiny room of my house on New Year's Day, my birthday.

I let the hours pass nodding to friends and acquaintances, most look like they've partied on through last night and are still going strong.

A few just want somewhere warm to crash 'til light. It's fine with me, tonight I am the host. I look out into the crowd of kids and wonder if someone here is cruising for me?

Am I on someone's wish list? The Beastie Boys come on and I stand in front of the sofa dancing just like I always do when I hear this song but this time there are people all around me.

Barbie gets up and joins me, so do a couple of boys from the sixth form and pretty soon there's a pile of us in the centre of the room, tables and chairs get knocked back with knees, and bottles kicked out of the way.

It looks like Barbie wants a chance to get closer but I dance myself around the sofa, looking for a way to avoid the risk of someone overhearing anything stupid she might say.

There's one of the girls from the advanced maths class here, I think her name is Natalie or Natasha or something.

'Hey Charles,' she calls 'how's your subtraction?' – that's what my class project is on, subtraction. When she says this she smiles and I smile back, at least I think I do, but she's already drifting to another part of the room. Barbie is on my tail so I follow after the maths girl who seems so relaxed in my house, it's like she lives here too.

When I catch up with her I'm not sure what I'm going to say because we're very different people. She's the kind of girl who can do your advanced algebra or help out with a tax return or memorise a credit card after seeing it three times. I'm the kind of boy to wear dresses and commits petty crimes. She's never around, in fact I don't think I've ever seen her out of uniform.

She looks pretty good. In the smoky room her skin is still all fresh and peachy. Even though I've never thought about her like this before, I start to do what I always do when looking at girls, think about fucking them.

If I'm still doing this after thirty seconds or so I start to think about how to make the daydream come true. It's like lust versus short attention span and it's a pretty good way of finding out if you're actually attracted to a girl or just plain horny.

So I try to imagine her on the desk in the mathematics lab, legs spread to reveal some soft white panties.

Probably cotton, isn't that what good girls wear? Obvious choice maybe, but still great, none the less. Now my hands are on her thighs, lifting that stupid regulation pleated skirt, about to get to the good stuff, I can almost smell her when my brain just cuts out. I can't do it. She's just too nice. What is wrong with me? First I get all teary eyed because Jack shows he's not a total cunt and then I can't even get going over this girl.

Barbie marches up to me, obscuring my prize view of Natasha and pretty much everything else and then goes on to tell me she likes my new hair and she wishes I'd cut it a few days earlier. *If I know what she means.* I throw her a scowl and try to move away but she has me cornered.

She talks about nothing, twisting her straight hair with a finger in what she imagines is a seductive manner. I think about burning her plastic face with an iron, pushing her down the stairs, stabbing her in the back with a kitchen knife.

No, stabbing her in the back, then pushing her down the stairs. Anything to get her out of my house, out of my life. She's just a risk now and I can't spend all my time waiting for her to drop the bomb on me and Jack.

I guess on the plus side I did leave her front door wide open, causing her to lose all earthy possessions. How could I ever have gone for her? When I click back into the conversation, she is still talking but I haven't heard a word, just imagined half a dozen ways more to get rid of her.

'Thanks Barbie,' I interrupt 'this conversation has really made me feel more like myself.' She's still standing in the centre of the room, mouth open as I reach the basement steps to my bedroom.

I want to check on the gun, it's like the gun is calling me. I picture it, nestled where I stored it under my bed this morning, in a shoe box, underneath two porn magazines and a pair of pants I stole from a girl's locker at school. I must be the only kid for miles who hides his secrets with porn.

'Hello again, Charles,' says the blonde on my bed. She's sitting cross legged, fingers tucked into the tops of her stripy purple socks, long blonde hair brushed to perfection.

The smile on her face is an advert for virginity, suburban youth and everything wholesome. I sit down next to her. I'm probably polluting her by just sitting this close.

'How are you doing?' I ask, then, 'What are you doing?'

'I'm just sitting on your bed. I thought that would have been obvious.'

There's not much I can say to this, so I just wait. I'm thinking about how below where she's sitting, just under about half a foot of mattress and wire bed frame is a box with a gun in it.

Thankfully before any of this can come out of my mouth she's started talking; 'Anyway, that's not important. What is important is it's your birthday. So here I am, right on time. Happy Birthday, Charles.' She pushes her flat chest out toward me, like it's a gift.

I wish she'd stop calling me Charles, it's like if she uses that name too many times then Papa will appear. Like the *Candyman*. Or *Beetlejuice*.

'Great, glad you could come.' I speak slowly, edging the words out one by one as she watches and slowly nods her head in approval.

She sticks her tongue out and on it are three cornflower blue pills. The tongue retracts and she sticks it out again, this time bare. Like a child proving she's taken her medicine.

I smile faintly, not sure what kind of reaction she wants. She's strange, but one thing is for sure, she's beautiful. Now I'm up close I can say it's not in the way that some girls are with nice legs or shiny hair, she's beautiful all over, even her pink tongue.

'Aren't you going to say thanks?' she asks.

'Sorry, what for?' Now I know I am not normally this polite, but I swear I am only putting up with this because I am confused by everything that comes out of her pretty mouth.

'I'm your birthday present.'
So there is a God. I let my eyes run over her body, something I've been trying not to do since I first found her on the bed and that's when I notice it. The gun. Tucked underneath her right thigh sits the weapon I stole the night before.

My mind falls through the possible scenarios: she's here to top herself, probably because she's fallen in love with me from a distance and now she's looking for the big finale.

What if she's going to shoot me then herself?
Unlikely.

If you're going to top yourself then someone else you can't rely on your friendly party host to provide a weapon. But it turns out Natasha isn't in love with me, she never will be.

Only it takes a while for that to sink in.

I've been staring at her, mute, for about thirty seconds.

'So if you're not going to thank me, aren't you going to at least ask me why I am here?'

'Ok,' I say, how bad can it be, 'why are you here?'

'I'm here to kill you.'

The grin on her face breaks and swinging toward me she holds my gun up and points it to my head, steady with both, hands like the police do on TV.

Twice in twenty four hours I've had this gun pointed at me. First by my best friend and now a total stranger. On my birthday. This was never covered in *The Wonder Years*.

I can actually feel it against my temple. It's a good thing we don't have expensive carpets after all because you'd never rescue them once they'd been covered in the brains of a teenage boy.

I close my eyes, take a deep breath. I don't even know if the gun is loaded. I should really check these things.

I could push her, wrestle her to the ground. Get my gun back.

Then again, I could die here, sweat coating my body. If only it had super hero properties to help me slip away.

SUPER SLICK BOY SAVED BY OWN SWEAT.

It's not going to happen.

'Please,' I whisper to no one in particular. Silence. I prize one eyelid back and this takes all my mental and physical strength.

Yes, she's still there and the gun is still imprinting a little 'o' into my forehead.

'Oh come on Charles.' Natasha laughs moving the gun away. 'It's not like it's real or anything.'

With my testicles still shrunk to the size of gobstoppers I stand up, taking the gun from Natasha's hands and slipping it under the bed.

Her hands feel cold and clean against the moist grime of my own. I place the gun back in the box, noticing both porn magazines have now been ripped.

When I look up from sliding the box back under the bed, Natasha's smile has returned.

'So what's your birthday wish Charles?' she asks and it's like we're both five.

'You.' I say, opening my eyes as wide as I can, digging my nails into my palm so my face flushes a little. If I try, I think I can just about make my eyes water. Girls love emotion.

She kicks off her shoes and lies on my bed. A big comedy yawn and I begin to think she wants to do it like when you play Mama and Papa in the Wendy House at first school.

I want more than a dry hump out of this.

I lean over her, trying not to think of how a few days earlier I was leaning over Barbie with the same intentions. Her eyes are glazing over and for a horrible moment I think she might want to play dead.

Who knows what these smart chicks are into?

'Those pills, they're making me sleepy.'

'Oh. Are they supposed to?' I stop leaning over her and watch as her eyes open then close then open again.

'I don't think so, Lucinda gave them to me, she got them from her Mum's cabinet.'

'You mean Barbie, right?' I ask. She lets out a big sigh, like she's told me a thousand times already that I should call Barbie by her real name.

'Yeah, her. We...know each other,' she mumbles. *Know each other* sounds like the kind of phrase separated couples use.

I picture the two of them huddled together talking or painting each other's toenails. It just doesn't fit, they're worlds apart.

The only time you'd see those two together would be in a porn film. The slender innocent blonde – probably in some kind of shackles and the wicked bad girl with dyed black hair and latex dress.

Of course Barbie would have to lose some weight but still, the idea of her straddling Natasha with a bright purple strap on, or better getting her to suck it, is good enough for me.

The thought of Natasha's pale pink lips around a plastic cock instantly gives me a hard on. I bet the whole of her is cream apart from her lips and nipples, both the same delicate pink. She's like the perfect Juliet, although I guess that makes me her Romeo and I'm not ready to die for her yet, not just yet.

Natasha's eyes are closed and when I nudge her firmly but in a way that could be accidental, her right arm flays into the air and she half shouts half dribbles for me to leave her alone.

The minutes pass and she still doesn't stir. I place my hand on her right breast, let it rest there. Already I'm bored of waiting for her to wake up. Upstairs, my birthday party is raging without me.

I count to seventeen before I leave Natasha. I was hoping to get to one hundred but I there's a big smash somewhere in the direction of the kitchen and go to find out what it was.

Some guys are standing in the back yard, maybe seven or eight of them. They're hurling beer bottles onto the common, then waiting, frozen still like that will help them hear the glass break. Jack is with them, but Barbie is nowhere to be seen. I want to find her, ask what those blue pills were, find out when Natasha will wake up.

Maybe even have a go at her for knocking out my best chance of getting laid tonight.

Downstairs is littered with kids sitting round, smoking and talking, playing dare games. I walk past a boy from the sixth form and hear him dare a girl I've never seen before to lick the rug. I'm not even sure I know what that means.

There's a few girls in the lounge moving frantically to the music and I'd like to think there's been a steady flux of kids dancing since I started it off a few hours before. Well, maybe you can't call it dancing, but wearing the carpet down with the grinding of their shoes.

The thought of getting laid is enough to make me venture upstairs to find Barbie in my quest to identify the blue pills.

Even though I know my parents are out, it still feels wrong to be breaking the rule of going in this part of the house.

My parent's bedroom door is shut. I press my ear against the white gloss, fingers poised on the doorknob, ready for some clue to who was behind the door, laying on the paisley bed, about to get rushed by an angry boy in a dress.

'I just need to get this first time out of the way and then it'll be fine.' The dull words come through the door and hit me like a punch in the stomach.

Her accomplice doesn't say anything.

I hear Barbie again, a low groan and then: 'I just don't want him in my memory for the rest of my life. You can understand that.' She sounds almost teary.

I don't listen for anymore, just stand in the hall feeling shocked that she duped me. Why am I surprised? She probably tricks people into taking her disposable Virginity weekly.

I guess this is how Jack would feel if he knew I'd fucked her to get back at him. Ouch. Bad move I know, but it's done and you can't take time back, can you?

I don't get to think about it anymore because Jack is at the top of the stairs, bottle in hand.

'What you doing up here, birthday girl?' he asks, shaking the bottle, which has some kind of murky brown liquid in it. Even he knows I'm not allowed upstairs.

'Nothing,' I answer, it's the best I can do right now. It seems good enough for Jack and as we walk down the stairs the sound of Barbie's climax fills the air.

We freeze and he turns to me, I avoid his eyes. For a moment I wonder if I should help protect the bloke she's fucking or join in with the beating I am sure Jack will give him.

'Sounds like someone's servicing your parent's bed. Must have been a while since that last went on in there, like fourteen years and three months?' he laughs. I smile, but it hurts my face.

Jack leads me to the kitchen table, where there are already several piles of cigarette ash mashed in food. He sweeps the debris away and produces in its place, two glasses and the murky brown bottle.

'My seawater,' he announces, but I recognise it, he's fed it to me before. It's a concoction of vodka, gin, water and whisky.

He once told a friend that he pisses a little in each bottle, like a signature. From the taste its believable.

A chance to bed down with my little maths tutor is looking less and less likely as Jack fills the glasses. The first one makes my mouth ache and my stomach churn. The second doesn't seem to have as much taste, like my tongue has already gone numb.

Now the room seems distant, the music foreign and the lyrics alien – I can't even recognise them as words. I can only understand the bass line, thumping steadily toward its destination.

Each drink I take Jack seems to match but when it comes to a third I clink the glass against my teeth and the contents spills over both of us.

A dark shape not unlike Japan appears on my dress. The mark on Jack's top looks more like Africa, or perhaps a heart, the medical kind, not the love heart.

We sit on the threadbare sofa and Jack bends down and sucks the liquid out of my dress, like a wild man removing snake poison from a wound.

I flush, but I don't feel embarrassed – maybe it's the drink.

My head is heavy and I think about Natasha lying on my bed, sedated and probably smelling delicious. I'd love to be curled up next to her right now, both of us naked, but when I breathe in instead of a sweet girl all I can smell is the smoke in Jack's hair and the Seawater in our clothes.

JULIET

Did you ever wonder what happens to your brain when you go to sleep? That moment between waking and sleeping has to be the most beautiful thing in the world. It's enough to stop people being afraid of death – that perfect fall as if your body isn't important anymore and your soul is free to wander into nothingness.

You get a different kind of freedom when you wake, the first few seconds of any day when you don't remember your own name or the night before, whose bed you are in or that you are alone.

The trouble for me is when I wake up often those seconds without recognition will turn to minutes, then hours. Sometimes whole days will be blocked out, fated to never return.

That party at Katie's house is still a blank.

As is the night Papa left and what I ate for dinner yesterday and now, added to that list is the end of my fifteenth birthday.

I can't remember how I got here, and this is the worst part, that feeling of uncertainty sometimes, it's enough to make me vomit.

The trick is to piece together the surroundings then work backward. I've read alcoholics do this after a night of binge drinking.

I am lying on my bed with no clothes on but the bed is made. I've woken because its cold, the window is wide open.

Natasha has gone.

When I touch my head there is no hair. There was a party in my house. I try on my *Columbo*, I go over the facts, waiting for them to mean something but tonight it's not working.

All I get are snippets of the night before, Barbie in my parent's bedroom, Jack's Seawater, Natasha, the Juliet in my bed.

I get right up to sitting on the couch, my brain in a rush but my body hesitant to comply, from there darkness. This is New Year's Day 1998 - my birthday. At least it was; the clock by my bed reads 5.15 am.
Everything is okay, I tell myself, actually say the words aloud – you've only lost a few hours. And I am right.

There are noises coming through the ceiling, someone walking in the kitchen. My first thought is that its kids left over from the party – the clunking sound is too loud for Matka.

I promised her the party would be over by four, an arbitrary time, so I can't see her getting too mad about some kids kicking about.

I follow the sounds of the steps across my ceiling and watch as the door to my bedroom opens. My body just lies there while some part of my brain tries to work out if I am bothered about Jack or Barbie or someone from the party seeing me naked.

Sickeningly, I feel paralyzed. From my bed I can just see the boots at the top of the stairs belonging to Papa.

He's in the house. Two nights in a row he's sought me out. What is he doing here? Why was he in the kitchen?

If he comes, he comes through my window. But that's not true. He's always in the room already. I just assume he comes in this way.

He must have a key to the house still, that's it. A key. Silly when you think about it really, you leave someone's home and you can easily get a copy of your old door key before you give the original back. Don't know why I didn't think of it before.

I screw my eyes up tight, hoping he'll go away, then try to relax my whole face so it looks like I am sleeping.

What kind of kid lies awake naked when his estranged Papa comes in the room?

'What happened to the house?' he asks without bothering to check if I am awake. I have to reply that don't know – which appears to be the mantra to my life right now.

Perhaps the house has been wrecked by some strange kids, perhaps it's still full of some strange kids. Why is life filled with some strange kids and never people I count as my friends?

Maybe Papa is just upset by the way Matka moved the kitchen table to a new spot. It could be anything, let's face it.

I'm still lying completely flat and he is standing over my bed. A few hours ago a pretty blonde girl was holding a gun to my head here, now I've got something even worse to deal with.

I half sit up but it's more like I am crawling backward on my elbows until my newly shaven skull hits the headboard. Great, now I am truly cornered. I look over to the far end of the room to avoid Papa's gaze and watch a shadow in the washroom rock back and forth.

I don't even think about what it could be, it's just something to focus on.

I wait for his next question, seeing as I couldn't offer a suitable answer to the first, but he doesn't say anything. He is staring at his naked fifteen year old son.

That must stump even the most abusive of parents, due to the weirdness factor alone. After the longest time he repeats the question: 'What happened to the house?' I take a breath and announce confidently, with no knowledge of what state the house is in, 'I had a party. It was my birthday, remember?'

The next part seems kind of blurred, because one minute I am lying naked on my bed and the next Papa is picking me up by what would be my shirt collar if I had clothes on and is shaking me.

A strange kind of rattling comes out from my throat and for once I'm not concerned about waking Matka, I'm just worried about breathing because his rough workman hands are clasped around my throat.

I've fantasised about something very similar for a long time, except in my version I am the one throttling some beautiful school girl and it feels good.

My heart promises to send a little private prayer that I'll say sorry to those girls in my fantasies as soon as I can, if I get out of this mess but of course, later when I can breathe again, I don't. It's still going on, this throttling, and I am surprised that my body is relaxed even if my throat is still making that noise.

There's nothing I can do but wait for Papa's strength to subside. It's easy to be calm when you know what happens next.

Stepping forward from the washroom is the most beautiful sight I've ever seen.

Natasha is now standing in the middle of my bedroom, entirely naked aside from a pair of small lavender sports socks. Her skin looks almost blue in the moonlight and I can see she is holding her breath. I could die right now, she's so stunning. Papa must be thinking the same thing. Even though his hands are still firmly gripped around my neck his eyes are on the young girl in front of him. Natasha goes to speak but it's hard to hear what she's saying, it's as if my seeing her body is muting all my other senses.

'Mr. Lewandowski?' Papa doesn't respond, just stares at her. 'Mr. Lewandowski, I'm Natasha, Charles' girlfriend.'

I can't say who is more shocked, Papa or me, but it's working.

Papa's hands creak open and my windpipe settles into place. 'I'm sorry about the mess Mr. Lewandowski, to your home I mean.'

She makes the word *home* glow and she smiles as if she's offering to personally lick the carpets to clean the mess.

He moves toward her, slowly as if trying to catch a mouse. I can almost see him hunching to appear smaller, less threatening.

'Why would you want to be with someone like my son? The boy's a faggot, you must know that.' She's not sure what to say to that one. God knows she's done enough for me already, like walking around naked in front of Papa. Part of me is imagining getting the gun from under the bed, not using it of course, just threatening him with it, then Natasha and I could run off somewhere warm where it's legal to have sex at our age.

The thought of the gun flashing through my brain is enough to make me feel nauseous and I clutch at my stomach.

Papa takes another step toward Natasha and the fear diverts from my safety to hers. In this situation I am useless, a bystander and observer only. It's down to Natasha to sort this one out.

Then it strikes me this is just like a rerun of Papa's attacks on Matka, if Matka were fifteen, naked, and in my bedroom.

'Wouldn't you rather meet a man instead of a boy, Natasha?' His voice is now so smooth I swear if you close your eyes you could melt into him.

She smiles coyly and he circles her body. She doesn't even shiver. Me, I'm a pile of goose-pimpled flesh and stale odour.

She just stands still, arms at her sides, her little pink nipples erect against the cool air. I know now one of us in this room is completely crazy. I just don't know which one.

'So?' Papa asks, skimming a finger over her cheek then holding her chin.

'Mr. Lewandowski,' She breaks the silence and her voice is so flat, so void of emotion it sounds dead. 'Do you know I just turned fourteen years old?' Papa snaps back his hand like she's fed him an electric shock.

'I'll drive you home,' his voice is all stern parent finding naked girl in his son's room. Gone is the predatory male. He shrugs off his brown trench coat and goes to cover her with it. I watch her take a sidestep as if she were avoiding the oncoming path of an unruly toddler.

'That's okay Mr. Lewandowski,' Natasha chirps. If she says his name one more time I'll scream. 'Charles has invited me to stay over, haven't you Charles?' they both look at me, but I can't see any emotion on their faces, not because of the dark but because they are both masking all emotion.

I nod gently, I can't disagree with her not now, not ever again.

Papa pulls back his coat, folds it over his arm and for the first time looks old. I think he's going to leave, defeated by a young naked girl but he turns to me and cups my face with both hands.

Our eyes meet and for one strange moment I think he may kiss me. Instead he turns my head and my neck with it, I feel a stabbing pain at the top of my spine and, exhausted, my knees buckle and he lets go.

Natasha doesn't even blink at this, in fact she doesn't move at all until Papa has climbed the steps and closed the door of my bedroom.

When the thudding of his feet across the kitchen lino ceases she goes into the washroom and picks up her clothes.

I climb into my bed, tired and sore. I can't face whatever it is that's been done to trash my house now, it will have to wait for the morning.

'So, are you going to ask me to stay or not?' she asks emerging with a little pile of clothes clutched to her chest.

'You don't want to make me a liar do you?' I nod in response and she climbs into bed next to me, still naked apart from those little socks.

Her tiny body grafts onto mine, a little bomb of heat curled up next to me. Her hair smells incredible.

'Thanks, you know, for everything.' I swallow.

Her hair smells like the first summer we came to England when I was seven and all the flowers were in bloom.

'It's nothing,' she says.

It's hard to believe this is the nerdy girl in my maths class, answering questions on calculus. Her head rests on my chest and we lie very still next to each other. Just as I am drifting into sleep she whispers: 'You're all I want, just wait until I tell Lucinda about this.'

Dr Partridge finds it hard to accept why I am in a bad mood this morning. He's getting annoyed that I won't sit down.

I try to explain that last night I went to sleep with an extremely attractive girl by my side and when I woke up, with Matka's breath in my face, she was gone. I tried explaining that Matka hadn't allowed me to see the 'damage' in our house until I'd come for my appointment in fear it may be distracted for the duration of my visit to the clinic. I then went on to explain that this, in fact, had just made me extremely agitated and not knowing was another reason for my unwillingness to sit down.

It's the second of January, 1998, a Thursday morning, and I am wasting it talking to a man in a tweed suit because he has a string of letters after his name and all I have are a string of blackouts.

When we were in the waiting room – which is bigger than the whole ground floor of our house, I counted his certificates. I got to thirteen before the doddery old receptionist called us into his room.

Next month I'm going to stroll right up to those bits of framed paper and read what they're for. I bet it'll be things like 'Perfect Attendance' or 'Marked Improvement' because no one can have that many qualifications.

I guess as doctors go, he's pretty good. He's a GP and a specialist doctor so no one minds their messed up kids going once a month when they can just pretend it's their limbs that are rotten, not their brains.

He'll also call you by your title if you like it, like you're an adult. I usually like it, mostly to see if he can say my name properly. After last night and listening to Natasha say Mr. Lewandowski a hundred times I don't think I feel like hearing any more *Lewandowskis* for a long time.

Dr Partridge has soft leather beanbags scattered about his office and finally I slouch in one of them, because my hangover tells me if my legs don't rest they'll make my stomach flip up the egg sandwich Matka fed me on the bus.

Today the beanbag is uncomfortable. My arms stick after only a minute as I sweat out the toxins of Jack's seawater. I spend the remaining time of our session peeling my arm off of the hot leather then carefully placing myself back in the original position.

Sometimes I think Partridge is more interested in my wearing girl's clothes than the fact I can't always recall events, or recall events correctly. Papa said when he was young that was called lying, Matka says it's better to think of it as my being an unreliable witness, sometimes I'm so busy looking out the window that I don't see what's happening right in front of me, so I don't take it in, or I just fill it in with what I think should be there.

Partridge is the only one who doesn't say anything, at least not to me, not yet. I am still being diagnosed. I say a prayer to the patron saint of mental health that I won't be coming here a year from now.

Partridge says I should tell him everything, but I don't. Not the important stuff. I never talk about Papa, but then I only started coming here after he left, so that seems right. Why talk about someone who isn't in your life anymore?

Today I tell him about the girls I've met since last month. I realise that Katie, Barbie and Natasha are all brand new editions in my life. I wonder if he'll think I made them up.

Partridge says it's interesting that whenever I'm *intimate* with a girl I seem to be thinking of something else, someone else, another fantasy.

I tell him I thought that was normal and he laughs saying it is after twenty years of marriage but not when it's the first time you're *intimate* with someone.

Then the buzzer goes off to say the next patient is here and he straightens the framed photo of his childless wife and looks away from me.

We get the number three bus back to the outskirts of the estate. Before we discuss the session, I tell Matka about all the new little gadgets and knickknacks in Dr Partridge's office that they give to kids who won't talk.

She smiles and makes little noises in all the right places. I do this because I think for some reason she enjoys hearing about it. Recently I've been thinking she does it because she thinks I do.

Either way we talk about it, that and the patterns on the doctor's suit jackets, which are all tweed. She still won't tell me what's happened to the house and I begin to imagine it's just a case of a few spilt beer cans and a handful or roaches in the garden.

The bus pulls up to the entrance to our estate. Three old women get on, one of whom nods at Matka. Behind them is Natasha. She spots us, smiles and as the bus pulls away, starts making her way to the back where we're seated.

She's wearing a hat and clutching a fluffy bag. It's the ugliest hat I've even seen but somehow she still manages to look beautiful. She sits one row in front of us, the bag resting on her knees like a little creature. I keep waiting for her to turn her head but as time passes, five minutes, then ten, I realise she isn't going to.

Matka nudges me and gives me the look usually reserved for men in pubs when an attractive woman walks past. I do my best to give her back a look that says *I know she's hot, but you'll have to wait until later to hear about it.* Being inexperienced about these things I am sure my look is more along the lines of *the jiggling of the bus makes me queasy.*

Our stop arrives and Matka stands, patting her skirt in shape like the driver will wait all day. As we rise, so does Natasha and she gestures to let Matka off first and she and I trail behind.

The driver looks considerably miffed in his mirror waiting for us to slowly walk down the aisle but when he sees its Matka he smiles. Out of pity, I'm sure.

Natasha walks with us all the way to the house and I can feel Matka growing tense as we get closer. The three of us talk in a forced polite tone and then I say nothing as Natasha ticks off every box on the imaginary form Matka created for my future wife.

Our house looks awful in the daylight and even though I know Natasha has seen it before, I feel embarrassed.

At night it's easier to stop your eye roaming over the cracks in the plaster, the patches of damp and that smell that goes with all council houses.

I know next to nothing about this girl, it could be that she lives in the same kind of dump, but somehow I don't want to believe that.

She's just too *clean*. I don't mean the ways she acts or what she says, I mean her actual body. Like her skin is scrubbed and soaked and moisturised every day, her hair is neat and brushed.

Her clothes are ironed and her socks match.

If she wanted to she could get a job at the beauty counter of a department store. Where they, like, *sell* beauty.

We're from different worlds.

With the key in the back door Matka turns, blocking the entrance. She explains briefly to us that now isn't a good time for Natasha to come in and I guess she's going to reveal the extent of the big mess.

At the end of her speech Matka turns to Natasha, expecting a nice polite goodbye from an accommodating girl.

Natasha pauses for a moment then, grabbing the door says, 'Oh I don't mind a little mess Mrs. Lewandowski, you should see my house.'

The three of us walk into the kitchen with Natasha in the lead. No one seems to question how exactly she got to be in that position or at least how she did without one of us trying to stop her.

Beer cans line the surfaces and the wooden table has a grey tinge to it. When I move closer I can see its just ash worked in.

Between the spilt bottles are little black circles where someone has put out a series of cigarettes. It looks like the table has the measles. I'm thinking it's not so bad, it could be worse. This is just the start. In the living room the sofa has a huge slash down the back, big enough to fit a person in.

The three of us stare into it, half expecting a student or an animal or a Dr Who monster to step out any moment.

'I'm sorry Mama,' I tell her and I mean it. These are her things. Even if they are old and smell of behind the iron curtain, they are hers and I've let them get ruined.

Her eyes are welling so I add, 'Really, I am, I swear I didn't expect this to happen.'

'That's not it love, there's more,' she says, toeing the rug where it's curled up. It looks like something has been pushed underneath it but no one has the strength to look right now.

It feel alien to walk up the stairs of my own home, at least with Matka. I've just never been allowed up here. I've got my own washroom and toilet in the basement, there's only my parent's room and a bathroom here. Foreign territory.

Matka opens the door of her room like an estate agent does and we walk in ahead of her. She just stands in the doorway waiting for our response.

'That fucking bitch, Barbie.' I have to stop myself from kicking something I am so angry. I figure after this happening taking my anger out on Matka's bed would be a bad idea.

On the wall opposite the window written in pink paint are the words *Charlie Sucks Cock*. No wonder Papa was so pissed off.

'Do you?' Natasha whispers to me and I think she's joking until I see her pretty face screwed up with confusion.

'No.' I shoot back and instantly she returns to normal. I don't know why I lied. Because I didn't like it when her face did that I guess.

'They must have got the paint from beneath the sink,' Matka says. Part of me thinks about explaining, but I'm just too tired. I've got a wall to scrub.

Natasha stays. She stays when I fill the bucket with hot water, when I throw in a sponge. She stays when I explain that Jack and I broke into Katie's house with the paint and how Jack and Barbie and I are kind of locked into this silly retaliation thing where we never discuss it face to face, just casually trash each other's homes.

In return she tells me about herself. While we work at cleaning I learn that she lives with her Dad, her Mum is dead. Her house is only slightly nicer than mine and she's no idea why she is so good at maths. Finally she tells me about her and Barbie.

'She's older than us, you know that right?' I said I didn't but I guess it made sense. 'She's been stealing from her Mum's medical supply for years. She's practically a junior junkie, seriously. She's never given me the wrong drug before.'

'Maybe you just drank more than you realised?' I suggest. Why I defend Barbie, even if it was in a roundabout, way is lost even on me. Natasha doesn't answer, she just takes the sponge which is now a kind of pink and grey ball of mush and starts to wipe the graffiti.

I spend a long time looking at the little bits of sponge that have gotten stuck and dried on the wall. Eventually she starts talking again.

'So, we're friends. Like I said, she's never done that before and we've known each other a long time.' For a second I wonder if Natasha has been sent to me from Barbie, maybe she's all clean on the outside but really rotten on the inside like Barbie was.

I dismiss that theory when I find they know each other because when Natasha's mum died, her dad started cleaning houses for extra money. One of them was

Barbie's. Any friendship based on such humiliation can't be that close.

This was long ago, Natasha says, maybe seven or eight years. Back when Barbie's parents lived together in a better house. Back when Natasha cried every night over the death of her mum.

I wonder faintly if she looked like her dead mum, then I think about what Natasha would look like crying. There is a moment round about then when I feel like maybe we are going to fall in love.

A trail of water runs from the sponge and down her arm, all the way to her elbow. I watch it hang there, getting ready to drop, but either she feels it or feels me looking there because her other hand moves across to wipe the liquid away.

'It doesn't have to be like this,' Natasha says. She means life doesn't have to be full of regret and sadness.

'We can right wrongs, change things, get our own back.' At the last one she smiles, a splitting grin that looks like someone has taken a knife and sliced her face from ear to ear.

Together we could come up with a plan. A plan to even things up with Barbie, a plan to shut up girls like Katie, a plan to get everyone that ever wronged us, maybe even Papa.

We'll survive on our own, one of us will learn to drive and we'll travel the country, doing whatever we please.

We're still sitting on the bed talking about it when Matka comes upstairs to tell me Natasha's dad has come to take her home.

At first, I don't know how it got late so quickly, then it hits me, it was her doing. She was filling up all the space in my life, eating up all the oxygen by just being here. I loved it; I knew already I wouldn't be able to be without her.

I beg Matka to let me go with her, just for one night, that's all I need. She gives me a look to say she knows exactly how long I need and what it is I want from

Natasha, but something about the pleading look on my face as I try desperately to manipulate her into letting me go makes her relent and I pack an overnight bag and head for a whole perfect night with the girl of my dreams.

Natasha's house is a maisonette in a concrete block.

There's a patch of grass outside, with a single tree. A massive number ten with a ceramic owl on top is stuck to the middle of their front door. Inside, the dark red carpets remind me of an Indian takeaway.

There's a distinct smell of potpourri which Matka always calls pough puree. How could the girl of my dreams grow up in a house that hasn't seen any new furniture after 1985?

This is the maisonette that was bought by Natasha's dad shortly after his wife died but there's still a vanity with perfumes in the master room, a wardrobe full of the dead woman's dresses, all neatly pressed, some still in plastic covers from their last trip to the dry cleaners.

This means that they moved house with the dead woman's clothes, unpacked them and put them on display in the wardrobe.

Natasha says one day she'll inherit them. I decide here and now to get her out of this crazy house before she grows another six inches and is able to turn into the living replica of her Mum. I've seen enough horror films to know she'll not want to leave by then.

I thank God that there's no basement for her dead Mum to be buried in.

It's weird, as grim as it first seems, within an hour or two, it's like I've never been anywhere but this dusty flat.

There are no drugs, there's no yapping endlessly about stupid things late into the night. This feels more like a girl's sleepover, with scheduled games and an assigned time for homework. We sit mostly in her room, her reading, me staring at her body or her touching my head where my hair used to be.

Things are calm until Natasha's dad finds her wet laundry from a week ago still in the washing machine. I can't help but smile. Even the conflicts in this house are trivial.

'Get over here and sort this mess.' Natasha's dad stands in the doorway of her bedroom, piles of sodden girl's clothes in his arms. He's larger than life, or at least larger than her. It's the first time I've seen him even slightly animated.

Through the mattress I feel her body tense, her back straighten. It's not fear she's showing us, its anger. When they first started shouting I didn't know what to do. I tried to stay out of the way, reminding myself not to mention it afterward in case she felt awkward, but it soon becomes clear this is a regular occurrence in their house.

Natasha hurls a series of obscenities at her dad and slides through the gap in the doorway beneath his armpit, running into the corridor.

I stayed on the bed, trying to smile softly when he glanced in my direction. He rolls his eyes, already tired. I can see the red around his eyes but he summons up all his energy to shout into the house instead of chasing after his daughter.

'Don't just run off, you little bag of shit,' he hollers into the spaces of the house where he thinks she might be. I look around the room, her blankets with tiny mice in ballet suits, a pile of maths books and *A Brief History of Time* which she'd told me was all about God.

In the corner are five balls of socks. Each ball a different shade of pink and purple, mostly stripy. They seem to have been discarded at the end of each day. I imagine her balling one after another, each day adding a new ball to the collection until her dad comes and takes them away.

Downstairs father and daughter are still arguing. I can hear their muffled insults circling beneath the floorboards, they slam doors a lot. Then a silence, followed by footfall thumping though the wide rooms, I can't tell who they belong to. Rustling, more stomping, then silence.

A minute later Natasha explodes into the room, red faced and victorious. Her dad ambles behind her, wheezing and redder than ever.

'*I* am not a bag of shit,' she announces and then lifting her arms high above her head she pours the contents of a thin white plastic bag – the kind you get at the grocers – onto the floor.

The stench hits me first, but I am frozen, all I can do is watch while in slow motion shit spills out of the bag, running in thick streams down her arms, splashing the three of us and oozing its way onto the carpet.

'*That* is a bag of shit.'

I've been at Natasha's house for less than four hours and already I'm wondering if my family is that weird after all.

Sure Matka is all flannel nightgowns and housebound from depression and Papa is a violent train wreck but I'm sure this kind of thing would never go at home.

'How did so much shit come out of such a small woman?' her dad asks me.

'Looks to me like she's made of shit.' I say.

Natasha smacks my arm with the back of her hand.

I carefully step back, letting the argument between the two of them continue without me, trying to breathe through my mouth until one or both of them lead the argument elsewhere and I can escape. But they don't move. The three of us stand around the splat of shit on the floor and I try to keep up with the argument in case one or both of them turn to me and ask my opinion. They don't.

I'm not even sure they remember I am here.

As it turns out I don't get to sleep next to Natasha in just her rolled up socks and I don't even get to see her ball those socks up and throw them in the corner.

The evening ends with me sleeping on a hard floor in a small room with a high ceiling. The plaster on the ceiling seems so far away, I feel like I've shrunken down to the size of a tin can. How can anyone miss a concrete basement? I even miss the cool of the walls and when I wake up it's the hot sweats that stop me going back to sleep.

Natasha and I meet several times in the night, getting up for a glass of water or one final brush of her perfect teeth. I keep trying to pluck up the courage to just ask her for a blow job but she's not that kind of girl, she just pretends to be.

Each time we meet the sound of her dad's body shifting against the springs in his mattress scares her and the object of my desires scuttles back to bed. It's going to be a long night.

In the hot room I run through the girls I've known and the ones I haven't but it does no good. Natasha is different, otherwise I'd just be able to pressure her into putting out and moving on. Maybe it is love.

This is the thought that makes the physical need inside me wilt away, until it's drowned completely in the fear that I'll never be able to live without her because this is love.

I still haven't slept when it starts to get light and I try one last attempt to rouse Natasha for a hall meeting by coughing, continually louder and louder outside her bedroom door.

When she doesn't reply I squeeze my hand on the doorframe and carefully push her door open. It doesn't squeak and I realise I am flinching in anticipation of getting caught.

One of her legs is poking out the side of her duvet and her foot twitches in little spasms. She must be lying on her front, but the rest of her body is obscured by her bedding so I can't tell.

She isn't making a sound, no breathing, no moaning – if it weren't for her body moving I might think she was dead.

I make little *psst* noises at where I think her head might be but she doesn't react. The girl must be a heavy sleeper. I push the door open further, deciding this is my moment with Natasha and she really wouldn't mind.

That's when the squeak comes, a big loud seesaw sound like you hear on Saturday morning TV when the geeky presenter gets something wrong.

I freeze, caught in the act of not having got anywhere yet, waiting to see what happens. From somewhere in the darkness behind me, Natasha's dad calls out her name. She still doesn't wake, she doesn't even stir. I don't know if he'll come out and investigate next, or if he'll settle and I decide all I can do is stand here in the darkness of the hall, maintaining the exact pressure on the door in case it makes another noise.

Nothing.

Time passes but I've no idea how long, it could be three minutes or fifteen. Occasionally Natasha's dad shifts his weight around and I imagine him trying to get back to sleep. How long does it take one man to drop off?

My calf is cramping up so I slowly step back, moving my weight onto my rear leg. I must have been standing in that position for longer than I realise because when I move my leg back my knee kind of disagrees and bends a different way because it's gone dead from the weird position. I can feel my body falling but there's nothing I can do about it, I let out a small yelp while trying to compose myself but it's no good. I'm on the floor, with cramp shooting up my leg.

Almost instantaneously two noises push into the darkness. One is Natasha calling out my name in such a sleepy sexy manner it's like I'm already in there, already inside her, and the other noise is her dad, once again, calling out to see what his daughter is up to.

Somehow Natasha, or at least her voice, is completely awake and she calls out to her father with complete clarity that she's just going to the toilet and to go back to sleep. He grumbles an acknowledgement and soon she's at the door, nearly tripping over me.

From Natasha's bedroom a pocket torch is shined in my eye and when I look closer, it's a luminous yellow plastic fish with a light coming out of its mouth.

Interrogation by plastic fish has never worried me very much and I begin to get up. That's when I see her properly. I sit back down again to get a full view. She's got on this tiny little fake silk kimono that ends at her thighs.

While I look up at her from the floor her hemline is level with my nose and I inhale as subtly as I can but I only catch that warm sleepy smell everyone has when they get out of bed, like a newborn kitten.

'What are you doing here?' she whispers sharply and for a second I think she's angry. I shrug, unsure of how to play it.

'Looking for you.' I tell her. She pulls a face because I forgot to whisper and ushers me up. Now we're standing I'm a lot taller than her, a few inches more and I could rest my chin on her head. Looking down the size difference doesn't end there. Our feet look like they belong to creatures from a different species. She looks so tiny with her milky skin and curled up toes. I yearn to go back to that night in my bedroom where she stood only in those little socks confronting Papa and changing my life.

'Your socks have gone,' I say. I guess it's a dumb thing to mention but it's what I'm thinking about.

'Yeah, they're over there.' And she points to a big pile of rolled up socks, maybe twice the number that were there earlier.

We're sitting on the floor of her bedroom, both of us with our legs spread, toes touching to make a diamond shape. We're rolling the balled socks back and forth, like a lazy game of catch and I'm wondering how she seems so great at night and so poor in the day.

In three hours we're going to have to get dressed and I'll have to head home, back to my normal life and eventually back to her ignoring me in maths class, but I know that is impossible and I just can't go.

This Christmas holiday has changed my life.

I'm fifteen, I must be ready to know what I want.

Then I see it before me, the perfect plan, Natasha and I will run away. We could go back to Poland, and I could get a job where my hands will grow calloused. Grab some clothes and the dead mum's jewellery and within the hour we'll be on the motorway, hitching toward a new life. Maybe I can even get Jack to give us a lift to the edge of town.

But when I look over to Natasha I know it's impossible. She needs her stability, her dad and their lazy arguments, her dead mother's memory and the promise one day she'll get to step into her mother's shoes.

Natasha needs her maths books and her chance at a real life. I'm just the lost boy she's interested in for a short time.

I'm going to be a footnote, an anecdote in the future that surprises her conservative friends.

She has no reason to run away. I try to downscale my plans, work things through one day at a time and maybe ask her if she wants to cancel her plans tomorrow and spend the day with me.

We could do normal teenager things like go to the beach, wrap up and grab a sand-filled burger.

I've stopped rolling the socks and Natasha must know something is wrong because she looks me in the eye and with all seriousness and not a gasp of the erotic she says to me, 'Let's have sex.' Like she's suggesting we go for a couple of rounds of *Hungry, Hungry Hippos*.

But for some reason we're both still sitting here, not moving. It's nearly light outside and I don't know why I'm not on top of her already. Wasn't that why I went to her room in the first place?

'Don't you want to?' she asks and when I look up at her face it looks like she's going to cry. I realise I haven't spoken since her proposal.

I just sit there as her toes curl and uncurl against mine. Her breath keeps getting caught inside her, these little wheeze noises I can't ignore but I can't do anything to comfort her either.

It's not that I don't want to.

Every bone in my body, especially the one in my jockeys, wants to get close to her and twenty four hours ago I would have killed just to get within inches of her body.

She's not just another girl. She's Natasha.

My Natasha. And even if she ends up a carbon copy of the dead mother and never leaves this town, even if she grows up to be a sour, pouting bitch, she'll always be the beautiful girl I know tonight.

A balled up pair of socks rolls toward me and I push it back. After a minute her little noises stop and I look up to survey the damage. We keep rolling the socks. Her eyes are pink and wet, the lashes clinging together, but she's smiling as much as she can. I think about saying sorry but the moment has passed.

It's almost light outside so I get up and head toward the shower with my rucksack full of possessions and lock the door behind me.

The shower is one of those ones inside a bath, the kind you find in houses too small for a separate unit. I strip quickly, but there's no reason to rush.

The water is cold and shows no sign of getting warmer but I step into the bath anyway, letting the liquid splutter out of the old metal showerhead and onto my body.

I'm still bruised and as my body stretches, it aches horribly. I don't realise when the water begins to heat, thinking it's just the constant burning pain radiating through my ribs. Soon, I begin to relax, let the liquid trickle over my neck, torso and down toward my stomach. My shoulders sink and my hand gravitates toward my cock.

The images of Natasha's body rush back into my mind as if she were with me. Knowing I could have had her makes me feel stupid, but the thought we are only separated by a wall drives me on. I steady myself with one hand against the tiled wall and it feels slippery and cold against my palm. Already the water is turning cold again and with it the moment is lost.

I'm not ready to get out and stand perfectly still, getting colder by the minute. I think of Matka, wonder how she is doing in the house alone, if her body is in a better state than mine. I worry about leaving her alone, in case she gets more bruises or she just disappears.

I remember once before, it happened. I came home from school and found Matka had gone. At first Papa joked saying she'd been hit by a car on the way to the shops and she was dead. I knew he couldn't be serious, if it had been true then family would be in the house, someone would have picked me up from school early. He wouldn't be watching the news with a beer. Something.

The evening grew later and when she still wasn't home I started to panic. He sent me to bed and I stayed awake for as long as I could, hoping to hear the sound of the front door clicking closed.

The next morning I got up and poured myself a bowl of cereal and waited for him to come downstairs.

I dressed in my uniform and watched the clock move closer and closer to assembly time. There was still no sign of either of them. I began to cry, both my parents had disappeared. It didn't occur to me to check their bedroom. Even as a young child I slept in the basement and knew that upstairs, especially my parent's bedroom, was out of bounds.

My crying woke Papa and he stumbled downstairs, his chin coated in stubble, shirt half on.

He was angry I couldn't take myself to school, but I was so pleased to see him I didn't ask any further questions about Matka. I'd just have to live without her, I decided.

In the playground I told my friends about the fate that had befallen Matka and somehow it got back to a teacher. When I was questioned, I confirmed what Papa had told me.

It seemed that he didn't realise I needed to be picked up from school either, so that evening when I arrived home thanks to one of my teachers, they were eager to talk about Papa's grief.

He explained that I had misunderstood and Matka was in fact, just in the hospital on a routine visit and would be home in a matter of days.

This is how I found out Matka wasn't dead.

It was a week later when she came home, limping and yellowed like rotten fruit. I never found out what had happened to put her there. She promised me then that she'd not leave me again and right up to now it'd been pretty true.

I get out of the shower, dry quickly, and peel a t-shirt and a pair of jeans out of my rucksack. They smell awful and the t-shirt is ripped at the shoulder, but something I would have once been picked on for isn't a problem now I've got a shaved head. In a weird way Papa has given me the ultimate protection from neighbourhood kids by taking away my hair.

When I leave the bathroom, Natasha darts in behind me, head down and silent.

I figure she's either just stopped crying or is about to cry some more. I don't understand women sometimes. If I cried every time a girl turned me down for sex, I'd always be in tears.

Natasha comes over to my house that afternoon, and we sit around talking rubbish. She's still pissed off about my saying I wouldn't sleep with her and in the end I go all quiet and coy and tell her I'm a Virgin.

After I say it, I'm worried she'll be able to tell I'm not somehow, but if she can, she doesn't let on.

'Don't you find it weird that people everywhere are, like, having sex, right now?' she asks, stroking my arm. I shrug. The phone rings. I leap to answer it.

Over the line I try to explain to Jack I can't come out to see him and Barbie and to be honest, even if it was him alone I don't know that I could say yes. Besides, he has been spending so much time with Barbie instead of me I wonder why I shouldn't do the same to him. A rush of paranoia hits me. Perhaps this is a test? If I avoid Barbie too much, he might wonder why.

I change my story, I explain that I'd like to go but I'm already with Natasha and after a few whispers in the background Jack points out his girlfriend knows my girlfriend and why don't we all go out together?

I relay this to Natasha, thinking she's still mad at Barbie over the drugs mix up, but she agrees and forty five minutes after I put the phone down the four of us are eating pizza in the local Turkish take away and I am crapping myself that at least one of my secrets is going to be revealed.

Before Christmas my life was pretty simple, or at least simpler than it is at this point. Jack and I would hang out, smoke weed in his bedroom and make money in any way we could think of.

If it was stupid or dangerous we generally gave it a try, because when it paid off, it paid off well. Now, everything has lost its balance and its shape. I have betrayed my closest friend, but not before he betrayed me. There are three new girls in my life, all of them crazy, some of them vengeful and the only one I haven't fucked is the one I want.

The four of us are sitting around over a couple of deep pan extra cheese and talking like we're in a Saturday afternoon soap. Natasha swings her legs back and forth under the table and I can hear the drumming of her boots against the boards of the booth. Jack is munching away, eyes down and I swear he's thinking only of his food and the next half hour of his life and in an odd way I can see why he's so content.

He's got a girlfriend who he thinks is devoted and faithful, a best friend who he thinks is devoted and faithful, not to mention very forgiving and now he's even got a reason not to feel guilty that he ignores said best friend, my new attachment, Natasha.

Even completely sober he is looking like a big smiling dumb dog. Now I can tell myself he has no idea of the secrets Barbie and I share or the years of on and off resentment built up between Barbie and Natasha.

Or maybe he does, maybe he knows everything and is just waiting for the effects of the last joint he smoked to wear off and then he'll pounce on us all. I doubt it and the string of melted cheese hanging from his chin seems to confirm he's pretty much where he wants to be and nothing is wrong.

Before leaving the house, Natasha had filled me in on just how angry she was about crashing out at my party, and that she blamed Barbie personally. She wanted to be on top form, she didn't realise I'd be so easy. I tried not to take it personally and she did say she meant she was worried I'd not even talk to her. It's pretty hard to ignore a girl when she's got a gun against your head. At least she didn't point it at my balls, everyone else seems keen on getting those first.

In the booth we are sitting girl boy girl boy. Between conversation Barbie's trainer etches its way across the leg of my jeans. I keep pulling back but each time I do she reaches further. It's like her stubby little legs are detaching from her hips in an effort to play footsie with me. One time she reaches so far I think that Natasha feels it too.

I scowl into my cola. I know she's only doing it to mess with me. Compared to me, she's got nothing to lose if Jack finds out about us, she'll just go and screw some other college boy.

When the pizza disappears Natasha and Barbie get up and go to the toilet together. I'll never understand how girls who claim to hate each other will still go to the toilet hand in hand.

Four bowls of ice-cream arrive and still the girls haven't returned. Jack and I devour ours within minutes, then watch as the contents of the girl's bowls melt into little pools of white slush.

There's a single cherry floating in Natasha's ice cream, like a little buoy all alone in a creamy sea.

The girls have been gone too long now and I vaguely begin to think about what they could be doing.

A small film at the back of my brain sees them fucking, clothes torn off and lips bitten and bruised. I'm the first to admit it's unlikely, but it helps to pass the time.

Jack and I are watching the lone cherry, waiting to see if it will sink, waiting for our dates to return. But in my head we've already walked out, left the girls and the bill, climbing into the Ford and forgetting about the craziness of the last few days.

As the engine barks into life I strain to see two silhouettes running into the car park against the yellow light of the snack bar.

Jack pops the cherry in his mouth just as Natasha steps into my line of vision. She slides in next to me, dabbing her red mouth with a tissue.

'Where's Barbie?' Jack asks but before she can answer

Barbie is tottering toward us and she is a mess. There are three red scratches across her left cheek, one of which has blood clotting on it. Her makeup is smudged and her hair is ruffled and looks almost wet.

'Well I'm really tired, shall we pay?' Natasha announces. Barbie is quick to agree. She gets out a big glittery purse and it keeps catching the light because she's shaking so much. I don't even try to look at Jack, I can feel the wall of rage that he's projecting toward both me and Natasha so I just keep my head down.

Within minutes the four of us are in the Ford on the way home.

I sit in the back with Natasha, partly to avoid Jack, partly to stop her from swiping out again. The tissue she keeps blotting her lips with is now bright red, like a poppy exploded on it.

Occasionally Natasha leans in toward me, whispers something that I don't catch and I wonder if it's an apology or the sound of victory. I'm sure Barbie will never get her drugs order wrong again, that's for sure.

Tinny reggae comes out over the speakers and she leans back into her seat, looking forward like nothing in the world is wrong, bleeding lips pressed tightly together. No one talks and every now and then I catch Jack's eye in the rear view mirror.

I've no idea what his expression means and I have to break eye contact and look down into my lap.

We slow down in a part of town I don't know so well, the large roads turning to smaller ones, trees appear and little signs for children crossing with them.

Soon enough we pull up outside a block of flats, the reggae whirrs to a stop and the engine dies.

Before I take any of this in Natasha's opened the back door and is standing on the pavement. She's shivering without a coat, clutching that ugly hat in her hands.

This must be her house. I know she's waiting for me to get out, join her but its miles away from my house, I doubt she's going to put out after last time and I've no way of getting home without Jack.

All these things are running through my thoughts and I still haven't made a decision. When I lean over and touch the handle of the door, she goes to smile, her face white and her lips too red like a geisha.

I want to smile back but my body has made a different decision - my fingers close round the clasp.

'I'll call you in the morning,' I announce and with that the door is closed and we're speeding off.

Already I'm regretting it. I turn to look out of the rear window and she's still there in the street, like she's in shock. I've left her, alone. I tell myself I won't wait till the morning to call her, I'll do it as soon as I get in, hell, I'll get my bike and cycle back round there if I have to.

Of course, I don't.

The next stop is Barbie's house and the both of them are out of the car before I can protest that I need a lift home. This time it is my turn to wait for an answer, looking lost.

I stand on the gravel, feeling slightly disgruntled. I abandoned Natasha for this, half an hour knocked off my journey? As he gets to the front door, Jack turns and asks if I'm coming in. I should try to patch things up with him and I'm grateful that he's not just going to walk off and leave me. Barbie looks a mess, I almost feel sorry for her.

Whatever the reason, I follow.

Inside the house looks exactly as it did before they were robbed, even the ugly sofa. When you think about it, it isn't that sofa but a clone of it, its cousin perhaps.

It's creepy the way the whole house is exactly how I left it, every detail replaced by a family with a seemingly photographic memory.

Did I really leave the door open? Was she really robbed?

I want to trace my fingers over the surface to prove that dust has had no time to settle here, everything is new.

When that grows tiresome I scan the room for a phone to call Natasha. I don't even know what her number is.

Before I can ask anyone about the phone or the dust Barbie is leading Jack upstairs by the hand and when he turns around his other hand is held out to me and it's good to feel wanted.

Barbie's bedroom not how I expected it to be at all. Rugs cover every available surface.

They cover the floor, overlapping in places so the ground is lumpy and easy to trip over and they hang on the walls making you feel that you're not in a room at all but some kind of tent. I sit on the bed, with a rug of its own, and try to count them. They are all different colours and yet all seem to be brown. Opposite the bed is a TV, on top of which are two wooden men, doing a little dance. It's too hot.

'Was your door locked when you got robbed?' I ask, 'This stuff doesn't look like it comes from Ikea.'

'No, I guess they just didn't want any of it.' Barbie frowns, like her stuff being rejected by burglars is a personal slight.

She disappears into another room.

Jack is on the floor skinning up a joint. He doesn't look up, doesn't speak. I'm actually relieved when Barbie comes back in. She's cleaned her make-up off and the three scratches seem to glow. I'd like to ask her what happened, but I can figure it out. This must be Natasha's payback for the pills at my party, or maybe for trashing my parent's bedroom.

If it were my girlfriend, mashed up in a state like that I'd want to know what was going on right away, but Jack doesn't even acknowledge her face.

Does he realise this kind of thing is part of Barbie's life or is he just used to seeing me get a beating that this seems normal to him too? Jack hands her the joint and as he does, his knuckles accidentally brush against her scratched face. She winces but puts on a brave smile for him. He doesn't react.

The TV goes on and the room fills with smoke. I lean against the wall, slouched on Barbie's giant bed, thinking about Natasha at home, what she's doing now, if she is angry. If I am now on her vengeance list. What she would think of me lying on Barbie's bed, would it make any difference if she knew I'd rather be lying on hers? Of course I could have been there, but what would her dad would think of that? What it must be like to have a normal parent?

Barbie and Jack are both on the floor in mid conversation. I have been daydreaming too long and am too far away to join in, so I just sit back and watch the TV screen. Either the set or the film is black and white, a woman slaps a man, then he slaps her back. It takes me a few minutes to realise that the mute is on.

The silent slapping continues until I'm passed another joint, or perhaps it's the same one. I keep thinking I'm going to drop it and focus hard on clenching my fingers.

When a person slits their wrist they lose all function in their fingers before they die. I look back the couple are chasing a man in black, maybe a vicar, through a very expensive room.

I lean over to pass the joint to Barbie and she's pulled her jumper off. Sitting in her skirt and bra she brings the joint up to her lips and I swear I can hear the paper rustle in her fingers as she inhales. I try to pull a face that might say I've never seen her body before. I can't turn to see if Jack appreciates this, I can't even turn to see if he's in the room. The straps of her bra are cutting into her shoulders. I can see the little pink marks on the white slabs of flesh, they seem the most beautiful thing about her.

The woman in the film is crying now, but it's okay because she doesn't seem to be that upset –in the very next scene she's dancing.

I want to call Natasha, let her know I should have stayed with her, stupid hat and all. I hate that hat. I am sure the woman on the TV would agree. She's off to find her lover now, at least that's what it seems.

Jack's face pulls into view. I am looking at his bare chest, how tanned his skin looks with dark nipples and the little metal rings that hang from them. He puts another joint between my lips and lights it for me. The end is wet and warm against my mouth and I run my tongue along the edge, feeling the roach and searching for some taste of saliva but the raw tobacco masks it. My lungs fill with hot smoke and it seems to spread through my body, edging up my shoulders and smothering my brain, drifting toward my mouth which opens to reveal a white cloud that joins the thick wave filling the top half of the room.

On the floor in front of me, blocking the black and white man from giving some kind of wedding speech are Jack and Barbie. She's lying down with him on all fours over her. Their bodies are barely touching.

She's in her underwear now, the loose pale flanks of her thighs looking almost translucent against the brown rugs. By thinking of them without their names it's easier to watch what is unfolding.

I know where it's going already. Despite our previous entanglement I've never seen this much of her body before and this feels kind of awkward but I've nowhere to go unless I get up and leave, walk the long walk home.

Believe me I'm sick of walking home from this girl's house. Besides, I don't know what time it is and my legs are numb, like there's a big dog asleep on them. Jack's jeans come down and with them his boxers, both hooked around his ankles.

His body seems far too large against hers, too long, too powerful. I suddenly feel aware of how in a few years I could develop into an adult white male, how I will do anything to stop it.

If I am male I am Papa. But there's no way to Peter Pan myself. The best I can hope for is Snow White, dead in a box, preserved to perfection for all to see and I'm not ready for that.

It's getting dark and with only the light of the TV to guide us, Jack and Barbie are half cast in shadows so they too seem black and white. All their flaws erased by the half-light, they look unreal. She's writhing around underneath him like she's possessed, her hips moving in little circles, chafing her skin on the rough mats beneath.

Her mouth is open, a string of spit connecting her top and bottom lip. I've never noticed before but her teeth are stained white, almost perfect.

Watching them together, all I can think of is how she didn't fuck me like that, how she wasn't consumed by some burning energy lying on my bed. Then why did she bother?

Why did she go to the effort, the risk to only lie on her back like a giant marshmallow with a bad haircut? She seems to be making a habit of it too, whoever she was within Matka's room wasn't me and it wasn't Jack.

I picture her on the hard double bed with flowery quilting. The bed where my parents once slept together. Where she spent the night of my fifteenth birthday pulling her *please take my vaginal Virginity* routine to some sap behind the door. I wish I'd looked, found out who she was screwing. We could start a club.

I don't need to picture anything though because she's there in front of me, a live sex show of my best friend and the girl I betrayed him for.

Suddenly a shot of colour bursts from the TV. It's the ad break. The light casts over their bodies, the green flooding across his thighs, the yellow on the arch of his back, highlighting the sweat that is collecting there. The screen shows a boy in muddy clothes chastised by his mother before being forced to strip for the sake of a detergent advert.

It's followed by a silver car in the orange desert, a family assembling furniture. After the black and white film, the brightness of the adverts almost hurt my eyes. The film starts up again and the room is plunged into dark grey again but neither Jack nor Barbie seems to notice.

The joint in the ashtray has gone out and when I go to pick it up my fingers are stiff. I pat the huge bed, feeling for a lighter in the darkened room, knowing it's not there. Jack's Zippo, the only lighter in the room I know of is tucked just under a pile of clothes Barbie is resting her head on.

I could get off the bed, lean over and reach it, the only threat of touching either of them is her arms raised slightly above her as if an invisible assailant is pinning her down. If she doesn't see me coming nearer she might wallop me by accident.

I roll the joint between my thumb and forefinger, trying to decide whether to do it. Before I can make any kind of decision consciously I'm on my feet, wobbling toward them. The uneven layer of rugs make me fall to my knees at just about the right distance away to slip my hand forward and reach the lighter. My fingers creep toward it, then clasping it in my palm I pull back. It's only now I see Barbie is watching me. Her eyes are dark and wet, like an animal's. Her right arm dangles near for a moment then she grabs my wrist and won't let go.

My instinct is to pull back – Jack's head buried deep in her shoulder, he won't see if I just twist her arm to make her let go but I can't. I look into her eyes, with what I hope is a sincere plea to be let go and with it her hand drops open, like she's died, and I'm released. Her hand stays in that open position and I see now the rest of her body is motionless, no longer responding to Jack's movements.

I will her with every ounce of my body to start moving again. Any moment Jack will look up and see me crouched over them. I should step back but all the blood in my knees has rushed to my head, making me feel hot and dizzy.

I'm sure if something doesn't change in the next minute I'll run out of oxygen and just collapse forward. But my throat doesn't close and my lungs don't stop working. I shakily edge myself back to the bed and relight the joint. Barbie keeps on staring at me, like a dead doll.

I get her point, he doesn't notice if she's a sex goddess or a blow up doll. She's still frozen when he finishes, his huge hands gripping at the rugs either side of her head.

I try to feel something, anything, as I watch my best friend come inside his girlfriend, but all can think of is how even at his most vulnerable his body is so physically strong. He could crush either of us if he wanted to.

What is most important is the lesson that Barbie has taught me about my best friend, something she was able to see in eight days I haven't in over a year, although why she has chosen to show me this weakness I don't know.

Jack gets up, leaving the room and she lies perfectly still on the floor. It's like he's been teleported off by aliens or something or has suddenly become invisible and she's carrying on having sex with him even though he's not there.

I move toward her, crawling on all fours because of the dizziness.

She doesn't divert her gaze into nothingness when I lean over her naked body, just lets a tear roll down her cheek.

I wipe it with a finger, tracing it back to its source. She asks me to fetch her white dressing gown, and I find it on the back of the door and pass it to her.

It's big and fluffy and the kind that when you see one in someone's home you can't help think they've stolen it from a hotel. She looks tiny bundled up inside the cloth.

'Are you going to say anything, about the other day?'

'What, when we had sex?' she asks, and I want to believe she's saying the actual words when her boyfriend is in the next room because she's stoned and not because she doesn't give a shit about anything.

'Are you?'

The two of us are sitting together in silence when Jack returns. Her scratches are still visible in the dim room and the tears make her face shine.

She huddles next to me on the bed, without really touching me, just jammed up like we're on a packed bus. Jack sits on the other side of me and the two of them begin talking over me.

Jack explains the Ford is due an MOT.

Barbie says her parents might be getting back together again. It's impossible to tell if this pleases her or not, it's just a fact she throws into the conversation. Jack mentions a band they like are coming to town next month.

Barbie talks about the Breatharian diet.

The normality of their conversation makes me feel even further away from them. One of them mentions my new hair.

Barbie begins to stroke my scalp which is now sharp and bristled from a few days' growth. It's kind of

143

comforting really. I try closing my eyes and imagine that it's Natasha's hands. I drift off to sleep between the two of them, dizzy and cramped.

UNIFORM

I don't want to discuss it. I don't even get how it happened. I mean, it's never happened before. Not that I remember, anyway.

Here's how it started: the Casio read 20:06, Matka was engrossed in the Sunday night highlights of *Crufts*. It was that bit where the small dogs run between the sticks, really fast, while their owners dash alongside them, trying to keep up.

The door goes off, a shrill ring that shocks us both. Makta, for once, doesn't want to get up. She can't get enough of those clever puppies. It's down to me. I haul myself off the sofa and I know what's coming before I even open the front door. I can see the blue light through the frosted glass.

Two of them, men. Ancient – thirty, maybe older.

I want to believe they're here about Charles, but no, their faces tell me all I need to know. They are here for me.

The police follow me into the living room. Matka is nowhere to be seen. They think I watch *Crufts* alone. Probably while furiously masturbating. I think of spit-stained Saint Bernards and blush.

The three of us stand, watching the footage for a few moments, and then I mute the telly and the dogs silently run in circles, the green glare of the Astroturf fuzzing the screen.

'Just a few questions.' I'm told. They look identical in their dark blue uniforms. Craggy faces, wrinkled from holding a perpetual expression of questioning. Eyes mute, like bouncers and border guards, schoolmasters. The only difference between them: one is blonde, one is grey.

Matka is summoned from where she's hiding in the kitchen and she perches on the arm of the sofa, refusing to reveal how much English she understands.

We sign some papers, confirming who we are.

We look compliant.

I practice my best neutral face that I learnt from *The Antiques Roadshow*.

Then it starts.

My heartbeat speeds up and my guts start to churn. The room shrinks, the walls, the ceiling. Matka gone, the police gone, the sofa eaten up underneath me, until only the glare of the TV remains. The rectangle of light dies out and I'm left in the darkness.

I'm in a swamp. I can barely breathe, the air is damp and fetid. I try to move, but my legs are weighed down. I can feel the swamp creeping up against my skin, my shins, my thighs. Somehow it's rising, climbing up against my back, I know I'm going to drown. I reach up, looking for someone to save me – Jack, Matka, even Papa. There is no one. I am alone in the darkness.

When I open my eyes, the blonde policeman is leaning over me. There is expression in his eyes – something between genuine fear and mild repulsion. It makes him look softer, younger. He rests his palm on my cheek, it feels hot and clammy.

My body jerks forward and instinctively my wrist is raised to check the Casio: only 20:24.

'You okay there, son?' Grey asks. He's standing a few away, peering in at me.

'Yes,' I say, 'I – I think so.' That's when I notice it – the warmth of the sofa is too thick, too wet.

I've shit myself.

The recognition on my face is enough to prompt Blonde to say, 'don't feel bad, son, it happens.'

ROMEO

It's not hard to find Jack. I walk over to the college campus and check for the Ford in the car park. The doors are locked so I sit on the bonnet, wishing I had a coat but trying to look impervious to the January chill.

It's completely dark when Jack arrives. I've been watching him by one of the classrooms, huddled up too close to another student. It's more likely he's selling weed than keeping warm.

He walks over to the Ford and I jump off the bonnet. He unlocks his door and gets in. There's a moment where he just sits in the driving seat, then he leans over and unlocks the passenger door. I climb in.

The engine starts and I jump as the vibrations run though the seats. I'm nervous, not knowing what to expect. The reggae sounds flat and tuneless. We drive into the night.

It's January 10th 1998, and Jack has 48 hours left alive.

'I got a visit from the police,' I announce to the car. I desperately want to open differently, something with more bravado. It just seems false.

'I know,' is all Jack says.

'They could come after you, if your prints are found upstairs or something.'

'I'll deal with it. I don't think it will be a problem, alright?'

'I'm sorry.' I want to say I didn't mean it, but of course, I did.

'Yeah.'

'I thought you left me at Barbie's, when she came over I was still mad.'

I sound petty, like a fucking kid, but I can't stop myself.

'So you fucked her? Jesus, Charlie, have you any idea how messed up she is right now?'

'What about me? What about the car park?'

'Yeah, well I didn't think it'd be that bad, okay?'

I want him to say more, to apologise properly, so I wait, I just don't say anything. My life is filled with these moments, just waiting to get more.

'Dude, do you think I wanted to see you get hurt? Christ.' I can hear the anger in his voice.

'Well what about the money?'

'What about it? I gave you half. More than half.'

'Then you took it back,' I shout. He looks at me then, for three maybe four seconds in which I wish he'd just look back at the road. But it's long enough to see he's telling the truth.

He says again how he needed the money to get away and the whole thing got to him more that he realised. How coming from a nice safe home sometimes means the bad stuff gets to you more.

He takes his hands off the wheel, steading it with his knees. His fingers dig into both pockets of his skinny jeans and he pulls out crumpled notes – tens and twenties and fives.

Maybe three hundred pounds in total. He dumps the notes in my lap. 'It's not enough,' he says, still reaching for more, but his pockets are empty.

No words. I let the money sit on me, like a pet. One of us calls Barbie a bitch. Jack swings the car around and I hold the dashboard with one hand. As he speeds up, the reggae tape comes to an end. Neither of us turn it over.

'Have Michael's family dropped the charges for the break in?'

'Yeah, think they just got the whole picture about him and Katie.' I say.

'Well, that's cool. I want to say I'm sorry, but I can't until you know the whole story.'

'So, what's the story?' I ask, although I know already we're heading to Barbie's, I've no idea what we'll find there.

'It's more complicated than you think.'

'What's happened?'

'I think you should hear it from her.'

I knock on the door and Jack waits just out of shot. Barbie's mother is home, she wants to check I'm healing ok, but there's no time to be nice. I can't help thinking that she's everything you'd expect in a nurse, she's all round and motherly, warm smiles and cold hands. How she gave birth to a prickly bitch like Barbie is a mystery.

Maybe her husband was a cactus.

I ask if Barbie is in and that's when she wedges herself in the door, leans close to me and asks if I am with Jack. I don't say anything because I've no idea what answer she wants. He obviously does and steps into view.

'Is Lucinda there please?' Jack asks. I wonder if when they're alone he calls her by her real name.

Her eyes move between the two of us, now we're both standing a bit too close to her. She looks over to the Ford parked at a jagged angle in the street. A decision has been made. She's not letting us in.

'I'm afraid she's out.' The nurse face comes up, stern but fair, it tries to say.

'Well, can we wait for her?' I try not to sound threatening, but I haven't slept all night and my empty stomach is beginning to eat itself.

I want to get this over with but I equally want to sit down and be offered some tea and maybe even a slice of buttered toast.

'No.'

I know this tactic. Matka uses it with telesales people. She's sure if you give no information then they'll have nothing to feed on and will have to leave you alone.

But students earning three pounds an hour are not the same as young angry almost-men.

'Why?' counters Jack.

'Because I said so.'

'Do you know when she'll be back?'

'No.'

'Do you know where she is, then?'

'No.'

'So you're telling me you don't know where your daughter is or when she'll be back?' Jack demands. That's when she shuts the door.

We walk back and sit in the Ford. Barbie could be anywhere, so there seems to be no point searching the whole town when she is probably in her loft.

If one of us had a father in the fire brigade we could get a long ladder and climb to the top of her house and look. It's a stupid idea really; the fire brigade don't have spare ladders.

In all the chaos I've not told Natasha where I am. If she called Matka when Papa was there, she'd have got a garbled or even totally fictional message.

I want to know what Papa is doing in the house so much, but there just isn't enough time to explore it now.

We have to get our priorities right and Natasha, like my parents, seems to be a problem that can be put on hold for the moment. Frozen until this issue is sorted out.

I haven't eaten since this morning so Jack takes me to the drive through McDonalds and we buy three meals each.

Jack is peeling open a Big Mac and tossing out the gherkins. Next he carefully pulls the patties away from the already melted plastic cheese. Not a lot of people realise that the gherkins aren't just thrown in. They are placed carefully on top of the beef patty, slightly touching – kissing, not humping.

'Do you love her?' I ask and he rolls down his window, throwing his first two slithers of gherkin out the window. They make a slapstick sound, like smacking a kid.

'Yeah, I do. Even though she's mental, I do.'

'Oh.' Even if I had the words to explain how I feel, my mouth is full of chicken burger. I let it sit there, half chewed in my mouth, enjoying the flavour.

'I've got to tell you something,' Jack says. This is it, this is the whole story. He could at least wait for me to finish my food.

'Barbie is pregnant.'
I want to be sick. Suddenly the food my body craved so badly just feels like warm crap. I let the bits of half chewed chicken and sesame seed bun roll out of my mouth and plop onto the paper bag. Half of it falls on the seat and I can feel a slither of wilted lettuce on my arms.

Right now, I might as well be that lettuce.
'Sorry.'

'What for? Fucking my girlfriend or spitting your dinner all over my car?' but he's laughing. Jack is actually laughing about it.

'It feels good to tell someone.'

'Is it yours?' He doesn't answer, 'is it mine?'

'I don't know.' He shrugs like I'm asking the time.

'How can she be pregnant? It's been like, what two weeks?'

'Look she says she's pregnant. Her mum's a fucking nurse.'

'But still -'

'Charlie, I saw her face. This isn't one of her games.'

'What's going to happen?' I ask. He is the eldest and this is his girlfriend one of us has supposedly impregnated.

'I don't know, we'll sort something out.'

I'm almost certain that Barbie's pregnancy is bullshit. I would bet my bike on it.

Even if she is pregnant then the chances of it being mine must be a million to one. In *War of the Worlds* they claim that the odds of any aliens turning up from Mars are a million to one. Considering how fucking bad that problem turns out to be, those a pretty high odds. That's what this is, my own personal alien invasion. Barbie and her spawn are invading my life.

Plus we'd have to wait until it comes out before we know whose it is. I can't even wait for a sixty second microwave Burrito to finish.

I eat another chicken burger - it's still slightly warm in the middle.

This chicken could have been someone's son.

I can't help thinking of all the sperm I've left in the world. On sheets and sinks, wiped into my jeans and encrusted onto my socks. Now every drop seems like some kind of toxic liquid that if left in the wrong place can ruin your life.

I want it all back, every last one.

'It'll be okay,' Jack says, tossing the second lot of gherkins out the window. We wait for the splat, but when none comes, Jack leans over and reports that the little discs stuck to the car door.

Jack starts the car and for some weird reason I put my seatbelt on. I think it's because there's a tiny, tiny chance I could be a father.

I've already experienced what it's like to feel like a rapist, this is the other end of the scale.

Despite the fact that it's probably all rubbish, and even if it isn't then it will be Jack's, there's this part of me that feels if I died tomorrow, I might leave something behind.

I can carry this with me, just a private little light inside of me.

Did Papa feel like this when he found out about Matka carrying me? I'd love to have seen Matka pregnant. She must have been beautiful.

When we reach my house Jack asks if he can come in with me. It's weird because I don't think I've ever heard him ask before, he's always just walked in after me or climbed through my window.

I unlock the front door and he follows.

It doesn't even occur to me that Papa will still be there.

My parents are both sitting on the sofa, Matka with a stiff back, hands placed in her lap and Charles, I mean Papa, lounging, feet on the coffee table.

They're both on the same sofa but you'd think they were in different worlds. When I come into the room Matka gives me this pleading apologetic look, like she couldn't prevent this happening. I bet they've been waiting for me for hours.

Jack sees Matka first and greets her, stooping down to kiss her cheek. It's only when he's about half way down does he acknowledge Papa, too late to turn back he goes in for the kiss. Matka flinches slightly and doesn't say anything.

Jack and I sit in a chair each, he's aware of how weird this situation is and perhaps it's even worse for him than it is for me.

One of us should talk but no one wants to start things off. Papa thinks he's building tension by remaining silent.

Matka has clearly had a couple of hours of the silent treatment and is unable to say anything without stuttering. Then Jack breaks the tension with the weirdest opener I've ever heard.

'Aren't you normally at work by now, Mr. Lewandowski?' Hearing this Papa turns his head toward Jack.

It looks like he doesn't move any other part of his body, like a killer owl.

'What?' is all Charles says.

'Well, don't you normally leave just before Charlie finishes school?'

How is it that everyone seems to know more about Papa's activities than me?

'I'll tell you why I'm not at work. Listen here. I'm not at work because one of you little shits has gone and got some *child* pregnant.'

'Touché,' Jack whispers.

I preferred the silence.

I can see the conversation going two ways, Jack will either freak out, shout at Papa to get back to work and leave or, he'll do what I'm doing which is sitting welded to the chair like a five year old whose just been caught stealing sweets.

Jack's lips are moving. I think he's cursing Papa, at least I'd like to think he is.

'It's true, Sir. We've both slept with Lucinda. I expect she'll still be pregnant after your night shift.'

'Oh you do, do you? You insolent bastard. What's that girl going to do?' I cringe. Everyone else holds their positions. 'Is this the little blonde?'

'Black hair,' Jack corrects, 'fringe,' and then, just to push it further, 'the blonde is Natasha, I can promise you I haven't slept with her, I don't even think Charlie has.'

Papa is stone-still, just waiting out Jack's words, but he doesn't stop. 'I think Barbie's the only girl we've both done, right Charlie?' and I'm sure Matka is picturing this is as some kind of weird threesome between Jack, myself and some innocent little flower.

'It's not what you think,' I tell Matka, facing her for the first time. She stares at her lap. She can't pretend not to know English to me.

'We don't even know if she's pregnant, it's only been two weeks,' someone says, and I realise it's me.

'Since what? Since you both fucked her?' Papa looks livid. The veins on his arms are visible.

'Actually, I'm fucking her regularly,' Jack stands up and moves toward the sofa.

For a second I think he's actually going to bend down and kiss Matka, but at the last moment he leans in toward Papa. So close I imagine they can smell each other's breath. 'I'm not your son.' The words push out from somewhere behind his teeth, 'you can't talk to me like that. Actually, you can't talk to him like that either. Come on Charlie, you can stay at mine.'

Jack swoops toward the front door but when he turns I am still sitting on my chair. I make eyes toward Matka, indicating to him that I can't leave her alone. Not after the bruises.

Jack just cocks his head in a sharp movement, the kind of thing people do to get their dogs to heel. I stand up unsteadily, the adrenaline is stopping my legs from working. If only there was a way to take her with me. To save her. But you can only rescue someone that wants to be saved.

I've taken a step toward the door when a heavy black thud makes contact with the back of my head. I know it must be Papa but I don't know what he's hit me with or how he managed to move so fast. Then I'm looking at the side of the sofa, how there's a clean patch by Matka's ankles and I realise I am on the floor.

My ear is filled with blood. It gurgles and gloops its way onto the carpet, preventing me from hearing the shouts above. I put my hands on the floor, palms flat like I'm trying to do a press up but nothing happens. My fingers dig into the scratchy carpet but I don't seem to be able to lift myself up.

An arm attached to someone swoops under me, tucking into my armpit. Papa sets me straight and actually brushes me down.

I can feel blood hanging from my earlobe. It feels strangely pleasant, like some kind of precious earring.

Matka moves toward me and with a single sweep Papa bats her away and she falls onto the sofa.

Suddenly, Jack, who I guess has been standing by the door, pulls Matka up and guides her by the elbow to the chair he was sitting in earlier.

I open my mouth, not even sure what I am planning to say, and that is when a wave of dizziness blinds me and I fall again.

This time I don't even remember hitting the floor.

I come round with Matka slapping my face and Jack gripping a bag of frozen sweetcorn.

'He's gone, sweet. I'm sorry,' Matka whispers to me. Her hands feel cold and dead against my cheeks. Jack moves into view and says something, but I can't catch the words. I grunt, curling my lip and he smiles, joking that I'm invincible.

I am propped up by the pair of them and Matka has the dishcloth against the side of my head. Every time I move to look around a whiff of bleach catches me.

'Bleach,' I croak.

'Hygienic,' she tells me and presses the damp cloth harder against my skin.

'So, what happened with this girl?' she asks. I know she knows Barbie's name but she doesn't use it. I mumble a few words about her being Jack's girlfriend and me being the bad guy.

He joins in after a while and we tut, gesture and generally use as few words as possible to get us through a clean version of the story.

'Well, if she is pregnant then both of you have a responsibility to her. Never mind who the biological Papa is. The two of you have been friends for a long time. The friendship is strong enough to handle this.' She proclaims.

Jack nods solemnly and I stifle the usual kind of protests after she gives me a speech.

It feels like a long time that the three of us sit together, talking about the future and how this baby is going to affect us all.

Matka tells a story of when she'd just given birth, how innocent I looked to her. I don't tell them that in the moments between unconsciousness and reality I thought I had woken up in a hospital.

The nurse was Barbie's mother. I kept asking her again and again if she had a daughter called Barbie but each time she shook her head.

I asked if she was about to become a grandmother. I promised myself that the next time she came in I'd use Barbie's real name.

But she didn't come back.

My new nurse is male. He is holding a baby.

Because I sleep through the day until lunch, I don't end up having to make a decision about whether to go into school or not.

Secretly I am relieved, it gives me more time to work out how to tell Natasha I could be the father of her nemesis' baby. It's not a situation I've had a great deal of experience in, so I tell myself there's no point going into school because it's past twelve and equally there's no point calling her house, as she'll be in class.

Later Jack will come round to see how I'm doing and I can get him to drive me to her house.

My nose tells me to head to the kitchen where Matka is preparing soup. The whiff of garlic and chicken hits me way before I get to the table. This recipe is one she used to make for me when I was small, it's for curing colds and the flu.

'Mum, I've been hit on the head, not given a virus,' I tell her at the same time as filling a bowl full to the brim of the hot soup. Something she's added, probably the garlic makes me hot and sweaty.

When I mention this Matka suggests it's helping to get rid of the fever I don't have. It's also helping me smell bad. I can't actually remember the last time I washed, I think it was at Natasha's house and that was days ago.

I walk the ten steps it takes to reach the sofa and turn the TV on. Sounds fills the house and Matka hums along to the theme tune to one of the soaps. There's a strange kind of happiness between us and I think we're both enjoying just being together. Then the doorbell rings, breaking our quiet afternoon. I try not to flinch when I think about it being Papa.

Matka and I freeze and I can see she is torn between answering the door and keeping social conventions or leaving it and doing what she wants.

'We could just not answer it,' I suggest.

She turns to look at me and a small smile starts to spread across her face. I mute the television and hold my breath, thinking somehow this will convince our visitor that no one is home.

'It's not like anyone would be home,' she whispers back to me. What Matka means is that she has no friends and all of my friends are at school. So it can't be anyone important. The doorbell rings again and Matka edges closer toward the door. I pull a face but it's no good.

'I'll just get rid of them, it won't take a moment.'

I turn the sound back on the TV and wait for Matka to come back to the sofa. It only half an hour until the quiz shows start.

When Matka doesn't return by the start of the next ad break I go and find out who is keeping her at the door. She's doing that bloody thing of just saying *no* to whatever questions the visitor asks.

It may have worked for Barbie's mum last night but it's not working for mine now. I head back toward the living room and that's when I hear Barbie's voice. She's pushed past Matka and is hurling herself toward me so fast I put my hands up by my head. She goes to pull my hands down and I step back just as Matka moves forward to intervene.

'What happened to your head?' she asks, her voice almost mustering concern.

'Just a bit of a misunderstanding.' I don't tell her that technically it's her fault I have a headache and an earful of dried blood.

She nods, her eyes wander around the living room and settle on the TV.

'Why are you here Barbie?'

'I heard you came over last night.'

'So you were in.'

'No, I needed to talk to a friend.'

'I'm surprised you have any right now.' She gives me a small, tight smile like she has all the answers and I think about what Jack would say if he knew she were here again.

I've got to get her out of the house, now.

'Jack knows about us.'

'Everybody knows about us, Charlie. It's old news.' A little image of Natasha pops into my head, I'm thankful she isn't included in the *everybody* that knows about the losing of my Virginity to Barbie. I really have to call her.

'So why are you here?' I ask again, letting out a huge sigh to let her know how I feel.

'I need to talk about the baby.' There it is, she's said it. Not foetus or pregnancy, but baby. A baby is one of those things you see in a pram, not the mush of matter that's been shot into her womb. A baby is something that is grown and kept and loved.

'When were you going to tell me?'

'I'm telling you now, aren't I?'

'Well, yeah but not before your boyfriend got to me.'

'Did Jack do this?' she says pointing to my head.

'No, but last week he pointed a gun at me and yesterday his actions brought the Police round. So I can say he was pretty fucking pissed.'

'Well, you did sleep with me. Besides he's annoyed because the baby is yours.' She drops this on me like she's talking about who owns a scarf or something.

I never paid attention in science class but I'm sure that in ten or eleven days a woman can't tell if she's pregnant and certainly can't tell who the Father is. Even though I know she must be bullshitting about knowing which of us is biologically responsible but it still doesn't stop the world shifting beneath my feet and I can't stop looking at where the thing that is invisible inside her is growing and how I need to protect it.

She's decided it's me.

'How do you know it's mine?' I ask.

'I just know, okay. It's complicated.' My mind races through possible reasons she'd have for saying this.

Is Jack secretly infertile? Does he have some kind of STD and won't fuck without protection, oh God, does she have an STD? Even if any of those were true, she could

161

still be sleeping with other men, she could have at any time.

'At my party, I heard you in my- ' I lower my voice so Matka can't hear 'you were in my parent's bedroom. I heard you with someone. Maybe he's the father.'

'Jack said you don't go upstairs in your house.'

'I don't, but only when my parents are in, it's like a house rule.'

'Well, it's not what you think.'

'Don't tell me it was Jack, either. He was with me.'

'I wasn't with anyone, Charlie.'

'I heard you using your line about being a Virgin. The same thing you said to me.'

'That's right, exactly the same. I was saying it to you. I was imagining I was with you okay?' She might as well have a glowing sign around her neck that reads *girls masturbate too*.

Matka gasps somewhere in the background.

'I don't believe you.' When I say this she looks down, lips pushed out into a sad little pout. She's waiting for her eyes to fill with water so when I apologise she can look up and two fat tears will roll down her two fat cheeks and all will be forgiven.

I don't apologise and she begins to cry audibly. Matka leaves her vigil at the front door and moves a step closer toward Barbie.

No one has bothered to shut the front door and I look out onto our street and the patch of grass and wonder what would happen if I just made a run for it and left all this shit behind.

'I love you Charlie,' she says, perfectly timed to coincide with Matka being in view. I bring my face in close to hers and she looks up, tilting her head like I might just kiss her.

'Bullshit,' I whisper.

The phone rings and Matka says something about it being like Piccadilly Circus in here and dashes off to answer it.

The front door remains open and Barbie and I are too tense to move. Matka calls me and asks that I come to the phone in the kitchen.

The fact she doesn't say who it is makes me realise it's Jack. I take the phone from her hand and move back into the lounge where I can keep an eye on Barbie and the gaping front door.

If she goes I want to see her leave.

'Is Lucinda there with you?' he asks and I don't answer because he might hang up before I can explain.

'She's in the same room as you, right?' I make some grunt of confirmation and for a moment I get to feel what it's like to be Matka when Papa is with her.

'She's just come from my house. She's going to tell you the baby is yours.' So it's true and he's calling to talk about it.

'She just told me the baby was definitely mine.' I can see the words leaving Jack's lips and travelling down the phone wire, entering my brain and making all the sweat on my body suddenly turn cold with fear.

I look over to Barbie, she's not saying anything. I've no idea if she can hear me.

'Dude, there's something else. She came over to mine first thing this morning to tell me and she'd come straight from that blonde girl's house.'

'Natasha?' I ask and as I look up, there she is in the doorway. It takes every bit of concentration I have not to just drop the phone and run to Natasha and try and explain.

No amount of words I've got are going to clean out the toxic shit Barbie has fed her through the night. I explain, half stumbling over my words to Jack what is going on and he agrees to jump in the Ford and head straight over. I've no idea if anyone is actually on my side, but I don't see what I can do about that.

Matka hangs back in the kitchen, her head down and her hands in the customary position of clutching some tea.

'We've got to go, my Dad's waiting for us,' Natasha announces. Of course she's not talking to me now, she's talking to Barbie.

I keep calling her name but Natasha won't look at me. I walk up to her, so it's like she's just dropped by and I've not yet let her in the front door.

I lean on the door frame, trying to look calm. My heart is beating so fast I can feel it in my ears.

'So is this why you wouldn't sleep with me? In case you got me pregnant too?'

'That's ridiculous,' I tell her. 'I didn't sleep with you because I love you.' Now it's out of my mouth I realise just how fucking stupid that sounds. 'I mean, I wanted it to be special.'

'Don't bother. Lucinda's told me everything.' I shoot a look at Barbie, wondering if I am the only one who doesn't call her Lucinda. I want to read her face, guess what lies she's said. But I am too stressed, too scared if I turn Natasha will have gone.

'Don't look at her like that, she just told me the truth.'

'What is the truth Natasha?'

'We have to go. We have to go, now.' I reach for her arm to stop her leaving.

'What's the truth?'

'You're mental Charlie. Loopy. Not right in the head. Fucking nuts. I'm sorry, but you are.' Natasha walks to the car. Barbie edges carefully past me like she's trying to avoid stepping in dog shit. It's futile and stupid but I can't stop myself from calling after her: 'Natasha, what does this mean?'

'It means I don't want to see you anymore.'

The two of them get in the back of the car together, Barbie clutching her invisible baby bump and Natasha staring out of the window, up at something I can't see. Finally, I watch Natasha's Dad, huffing like a tired old dog as he puts his car into gear and drives away.

When Jack arrives at my house he has only six hours to live. He doesn't know that of course, neither do I. It seems stupid that we spend the last day of his life sitting at the back of my house, discussing our plans for the future. What a waste of time.

Jack is sure all Barbie needs to do is have an abortion then after that we can all sit down and work out if we're going to ever speak again. Until that's sorted out, he says he can't begin to think about his relationship with her or with me.

For now all we can do is wait for her decision and carry on with our lives. In limbo. It's funny, but I didn't even consider the idea that she'd have an abortion. Perhaps because if she did the problem would go away and that's just not what Barbie wants.

After three bottles of beer we decide to drive down to the off license to pick up some more, but when we get there the place is closed. We try another one, a little further away. In the Ford it's only a five minute trip.

We circle the whole of town and there isn't a single place open to buy alcohol. It's like a really shit episode of the *Twilight Zone*. The one where all the beer went.

We end up parked by the beach, watching the yellow streetlights warm the domes of the pier. Every other summer some kid dies from jumping off the end when the tide is out. Serves them right for being so stupid if you ask me.

The waves are so loud tonight that it feels like they're crashing against the body of the Ford. We're sitting in silence and it almost feels as if the last two weeks haven't happened at all.

Midnight comes and goes.

It's crazy to think it's a school night and across town people like Katie are ironing their shirts and packing their lunches and even though I am just around the corner from their houses I am living in another world now and I don't know if I will ever get to go back.

It's starting to get cold without the engine running and Jack suggests we go for a drive. Even at this point I have an idea that he's pretty drunk and thinking about going to Barbie's.

I don't protest and we drive along the seafront until all the pools of yellow light disappear and we're back into the estate. The nearer we get to Barbie's house the more I think about suggesting we head home, but the words never seem to come out of my mouth.

Sitting outside Barbie's house, with beer and bewilderment in my belly it seems like a great idea to storm inside and demand to know which one of us is the Father of her unborn child. It's as if we pressure her enough she can wiggle her fall-open tubes and her baby will be magnetically drawn to the sperm donor.

When we go, we go quickly. Parked outside there was always the option of turning back, but now we are out of the car, doors opening together and storming toward the house in one synchronised movement as if we'd rehearsed it a thousand times before.

At the door we knock, don't ring the bell, but let the thud of knuckle against wood echo through the house. Like you see on the best police shows.

A light goes on somewhere upstairs and we wait. It's January and I don't have a coat on. I should be freezing but the adrenaline is keeping me warm, like there's petrol burning through my veins.

The door opens and it's not Barbie or her mother, but a short man. It takes me a second to realise we're at the right house and there must be other people in her life that I just don't know about.

Maybe this is her dad and he's joined the family again. The short man stares at us and I try to work a charming sentence out of my mouth but before I can reason our way through the door Jack barges past the short man and heads upstairs.

I hesitate for a second, but follow Jack because if I don't I'll lose my momentum and realise how stupid what we're doing is.

Inside Barbie's bedroom it's so hot I think I'm going to be sick. When I reach the doorway Jack's hand is already inches from Barbie's face.

It looks like he's trying to touch her, maybe outline the shape of her face with his fingertips but if he does then she'll burn him, so instead he hovers near her, not daring to touch, but it's useless as she's already burned him.

They're standing in the centre of the tiny attic room, eyes locked, with only Jack's hand separating their faces. This, more than any other moment, is when I realise that he loves her. That means that he's been betrayed twice, once by his best friend and once by his lover. I look back on the last two weeks and wonder what his story would sound like.

I don't understand how he isn't angry at me, isn't blaming me right now, but I don't even think he can see I'm in the room.

Barbie is clutching her stomach, an action she's been doing all day.

It's like an instinct she's learned to protect the life inside of her. I look again at the flat place where soon a baby will grow and grow until it's ready to burst out. Jack will never see it happen. Neither will I.

Jack's fingers meet with the marks on Barbie's face. The three strips Natasha gave her are healing well, I couldn't even see them earlier, but now they've risen, as if to meet Jack and he's touching them so tenderly it seems he's afraid Barbie might break.

Jack is crying, I don't think I've ever seen him cry before, not even when Judy came back from university all messed up.

It seems wrong to be watching this private moment between them, so I look around the room, staring at the collection of brown rugs, the window, bits of paper on the side.

On Barbie's bedroom door is a small red heart with a black and white photo of a couple from the past. There's some writing across the image. It says *I love Lucy*. I guess she sees herself as Lucy.

I tell myself if things go well, or even if things just turn out all right I'll stop calling her Barbie, start using her real name. Be a bit nicer.

It seems obvious now that whoever is the biological father of this baby, Jack will step up and become the acknowledged dad, the least I can do is start using Barbie's real name. Maybe the baby will be all of ours, something to tie Jack and I together forever.

I try to imagine this room with a baby crying in it. A cot where the beauty cabinet stands, a plastic sheet over the TV to change nappies on.

I know nothing about children.

I look up at them again, wondering if I should leave them to it and use the long walk home to sober me up. It's still a school day tomorrow.

A flash of facing Natasha in maths class tomorrow hits me but I let it pass, I don't have to deal with it for another twelve hours and that's a long time in a teenage boy's life.

Who knows what could happen by then?

I can't hear their conversation but their faces are looking distorted. Barbie is trying to explain something to Jack, her hands held out in front of her, palms up as if in prayer. He's shaking his head, both hands still firmly planted on her shoulders.

As his head moves the light catches it and the streaks of his tears make his face shine like he's made of plastic. I keep thinking I should step in, or at least move closer to take in what they're saying, but I don't. I think it's the urge to be the person nearest to the exit because under the fog of my brain I can feel when we leave, we're going to be doing it in a hurry.

Out of their whispers Barbie shouts that she *doesn't want to*. I haven't heard anything else but I don't need to. Jack shushes her, looking back at me like I might intervene. I don't do anything. Not tonight, anyway.

The whispering creeps up to talking then shouts within a minute. Jack takes one hand from Barbie's shoulder and sharply slaps her face the way someone swats a fly. Immediately, or at least before she can move away, his hand goes back to her shoulder.

That's when I realise she doesn't want to be there. He's holding her in place.

She looks over to me and says my name. I move a step closer but stop as soon as Jack makes eye contact with me. If she is hysterical then he is a mad man. This is the only bit of the conversation I hear.

'There isn't a choice anymore. We have to sort this out.'

'This isn't cleaning up a stain. This is our child.'

I automatically feel included in this statement, like the baby was created by the three of us equally. And maybe that guy she was with at my party. Because there must have been a guy. I don't buy that she was alone for a second.

'Are you going to sort it out Lucinda?' but she only whines in response. She looks tired being held in place, her knees keep bending.

'Are you Lucy?' She squeals a bit and shakes her shoulder. Then she calls out 'Daddy!' really loud. At first I think she's trying to appeal to Jack's soft side, it's only later I realise that the little man downstairs is her father.

When she shouts, instead of letting her go Jack pushes her.

It didn't seem that big a movement, he just flicks his wrists and Barbie falls back, and as she falls she hits her head on the edge of the TV. The statue of the two dancing men fall on top of her.

'We've got to go.' Jack tells me.

I knew I should have stayed by the door.

I want to go, know that the small man could be coming up the stairs any moment, but I can't leave. Not because Barbie is hurt, but because she's carrying our child. The child. The child that connects the three of us, the child that binds me and Jack forever.

Maybe Barbie is just the carry case, maybe it's what's inside her that's important.

I move closer to her, as close as I dare. Leaning down I put my cheek next to her mouth, I can't tell if she's still breathing and the rug under my hand is wet. I can't bring myself to look at it and find out if it's blood.

Jack shouts my name and I wake up. We bound down the stairs, almost tripping over each other. I keep telling myself she'll be okay. Papa did a similar thing to me and I was fine. But hitting your head is a weird thing. She could die, she could turn into a spazz or she could lose her baby. My baby. Our baby.

But I guess that was the point.

I'd like to say that our running down the stairs brought the little man out of whatever room he was in and he would investigate what the noise was, or that he heard Barbie shout and went to check on her and make sure she was fine. But I just don't know that.

He didn't come when we bust into the house, just went back to the TV show he was glued to, he didn't hear her scream for him either.

My legs seem to be working on their own and we're fine until I get to the bottom of the stairs and Jack can't open the catch on the front door. His fingers look like the size of uncooked sausages. A siren passes somewhere in the neighbourhood and even though I know it can't be connected to us, I panic and put both my hands on Jack's back, like I can give him the skill to open the door and if not just push him right through it.

It doesn't work and when I take my hands away I see the dark, almost black imprint on his white shirt of Barbie's blood. A noise jumps from the inside of my throat and I push Jack out the way, opening the latch on the first attempt and running to the Ford.

ECHO

The air outside is cold and damp, it's such a contrast to the heat of Barbie's room I nearly stop still but the siren can still be heard and we bundle into the car.

I look at my hand. The one covered in Barbie's blood. I look back to her house, like somehow I'll be able to gauge whether she's safe now.

Jack starts the Ford and I thank every God I can think of that he's able to turn the ignition and start to drive.

He leans over me, opening the glove compartment and I half expect him to pull out a gun but he reaches in and pulls out three tapes in his hand. He shakes two of them off and shoves the remaining one in the tape player. He shoves it in and after a short whirr the tape spins to life. But instead of Bob Marley or Eddie Grant a rush of the dance music hits the back speakers and the bass is so intense it feels like it shakes the imitation leather seats.

Jack's foot pushes down on the accelerator and the scenery starts to blur. Neither of us have said anything since we got in the car.

I'd like to think it's the music that's making him speed way too fast up the motorway, but I'm pretty sure it's the fact he may have just offed his pregnant girlfriend.

I don't know how he can be so calm. Every time we pass under a street light and I see the inky print of Barbie's blood on my hand panic rises in my throat and I have to fight it down.

I know if I don't I'll just open the door of the car while we're moving and tumble out. I put my seatbelt on and turn to Jack. He's got his eyes on the road, we're on the motorway.

The blood on me is drying and I try to remember if it felt warm when I put my hand in it.

The way blood comes out of someone's body is so weird; suddenly we all seem so fragile, so breakable. She just spilt, right onto the carpet.

The straight lines of the road are almost hypnotic and the further we travel from Barbie's house the easier it becomes to breathe. At some point in our journey Jack turns the music down and looks at me. I think he's going to talk about the baby, or ask me if I think Barbie is okay.

He doesn't.

He says we'll just drive a bit further up the motorway and then turn around. I nod, a clear sharp movement to let him know I'm on his side.

He tells me this album is Judy's, that she left it in the Ford a couple of days ago and she's been clean from heroin for a nearly week.

Jack even let her drive some of the way home from the clinic. That's when she left the tape in the car.

Jack jokes about all the spare money he'll have now he won't have to pay for her addiction. He might even give up dealing weed at college. He tells me he's thinking of taking her somewhere nice for the summer, a weekend away somewhere. Camping or something. Maybe I'd like to come, if the problem gets resolved. Again, I nod, beginning to feel like one of those dogs in the backs of cars nicer than this one.

I keep waiting for him to mention Barbie, but we just keep going, up the never-ending motorway.

The signs change to the names of places I don't know and because I don't drive I don't even know if we've changed direction.

Finally, just before dawn Jack starts to talk. He talks me into believing Barbie will be fine, that people bleed easily from their heads and I'd lost more the night before.

I think of the thick sticky blood and how it was hot inside my ear.

Jack goes on to tell me someone would take her to the hospital for an x-ray and she'd get better care than me with Matka's cold dishcloth against my head to bring the bump out.

The smell of bleach wafts through my memory and causes me to wrinkle my nose.

I ask Jack what we're going to do, he's the older one after all. We talk about our options, making an anonymous 999 call from the side of the road, calling Judy or one of our parents and asking them to check on things without the police getting involved or, my favourite, driving to a big city and starting again.

Jack even promises that we'll turn around at the next junction and if we're not home before morning then we can stop off at the services and check she's okay.

I didn't ask for any of this but I think it makes him happier to feed me this information, comforting himself in the process.

I want to ask him if we can keep the baby, the way a kid asks his mum for a rabbit.

I don't, instead, I close my eyes.

When I open them the sun is rising in an orange hue of pollution that stretches over the horizon. Suddenly there is traffic on the road, noises from cars outside, and the dance hit of the summer blaring out of the tape-deck.

The windows have been opened and a sharp chill rides up my bare arms and coasts over my body until it hits my brain, giving me an instant headache. I'm sure it's the cold that's woken me up.

The woman on the tape deck has no idea she's singing to two hopeless teenagers, all she wants is to see the sun shine. That's what makes me realise what is wrong.

In the bonnet of the Ford the reflections of the other cars and the trees on the embankment dance easily. A peaceful moment, this would make a beautiful memory if it weren't for the fact it were ten times too slow. We are skidding now, me and Jack and the Ford and the images on the bonnet are no longer dancing but sliding, distorted, out of view.

I open my mouth to shout but nothing comes out or if it does, I don't hear it. I look over at Jack and see my hand grabbing his arm. His head jerks up, his chin rises from his chest like someone has given him an electric shock.

I know already that he's woken up too late.

That's when it starts; my life actually begins to flash before my eyes, just like TV always promised. But the real thing isn't like my memory, which is a series of blurry snapshots, it's a crystal-clear picture played out like a film, in glorious fucking Tech-ne-colour. Every detail is here. The whole fifteen years muddled up and spitting itself out in any order the back parts of my brain will allow.

I'm on the lawn, barely six months old with the sun in my face and Matka leaning over me, pulling a soft cotton hat over my eyes, then it's five years later and it's the first time I was attacked at school, I'm pressed against the cold wet tiles of the toilet floor with some kid's boot making a print on my almost-white school shirt.

Then I've skipped to just a few days ago, heaving against Barbie's body, the smell of cough mixture in my nose and back to visiting Matka in hospital when I was still too small to see over the bed.

The memories come faster; trying on Judy's underwear, shoplifting designer stilettos, eating salt until I vomited on the sofa. Katie on the lawn and that precious taste of freedom. Leaving Matka at the kitchen table crying. Natasha naked, Natasha broken-hearted, Natasha with a gun in her fragile hands. The night Papa left after hitting me with his spanner.

Then a thousand Friday nights, exactly the same, reeling out behind me like the cat's eye on this motorway and every night, good and bad, having Jack beside me, my only friend, my love, my chauffer this morning, driving me into the tarmac with him.

When we smash into the central reservation, the front driver's side crunches up and sparks and smokes and spits bits of metal and despite Jack's hands being locked onto the steering wheel, the rear of the Ford spins around so we end up facing the wrong way and then it seems like the Ford has stopped but we're still moving forward.

There's an impact and then we grind to a halt, followed by that silence, the first thing my senses tune back into is the woman on the tape, the same woman as before is now interested in a silver lining. She can fuck off, I don't think any of us are going to find one of those today.

I am aware of a man standing outside my window and for a second it seems completely logical that it would be Jack. I turn to face him, my mouth warped into a smile so big I can feel the wind on my gums, and it's a paramedic.

He asks if I'm okay and I nod, looking down at my seatbelt, the belt I never normally wear. He tells me we have to help my friend and I look over to Jack, but Jack isn't there anymore.

The traffic around us stops and starts, and I sit patiently as horns are beeping and the sounds of the pop song continue to creep out of the tape and they remove Jack's body from the Ford.

A nurse informs me that I'm lucky to have a shaved head, because if I hadn't they wouldn't have been able to see how deep the cuts were and then they'd have had to shave sections of my hair off, like you sometimes see on animals when they have an injection at the vets.

I nod, because that's all I can manage. I don't feel very lucky, I feel like I've died as well, except that while my brain is numb, my body is still moving and breathing, unlike Jack's. I've been told that's shock and the drugs I've been given.

The paramedic that asked me if I was okay, the same one that found the cuts on my head and later helped pull Jack's body from the car took me to the local hospital in one ambulance and then sent for another to pick up Jack.

There was a second paramedic, the one whose job it was to stay with Jack I guess, or to stay with his body, but he didn't talk to me.

They took me to the children's ward of our local hospital, I don't recognise it from the inside but then one of the nurses looks up my records and tells me I was born four floors down.

This means that if Jack had kept awake for twenty minutes longer, or if we'd turned back ten minutes earlier we would have reached home.

I don't say this to anyone, there's no one to say it to. I am waiting for the grey out, for the point my brain can't take anymore and it shuts down and lets me forget all of this but it doesn't come.

There's a window behind my bed and a square of cold January sun is hitting the wall, bleaching out the animal print of the wallpaper and reminding everyone that the world is still moving.

After several hours, the Police arrive with a doctor, the special head kind, not the body kind. It's nearly lunch and the corridor is filling up with that hospital smell of disinfectant, mash and meat.

The police decide to hold back my lunch until I talk to them, which seems crazy to me. I've just been in a major accident, one that has killed my best friend and they think they can negotiate information out of me by keeping back a meal.

What they do have, that I crave for more than anything I've craved before, more than my stomach wrestles for food, even more than Judy needs her smack, is to find out if Jack died a sinner or a saint. I need to know about Barbie.

They want me to tell them the whole thing before they'll give me any information about Barbie. They want every detail and I give it to them, just as I have here, right down to the lyrics coming from the tape at the end and I hope where ever he is Jack forgives me for telling the police that he died to a pop song, but I won't let the world find that out.

After recounting everything they bring me my meal, which has been sitting on a tray in the hall from the time I started to tell the story.

I shovel in a forkful of cold pie and one of the policemen tells me about Barbie. I wonder if they're expecting me to spit my food out when I hear what they have to say.

Around the time we run out of Barbie's house, slamming the door behind us, the channel Barbie's father is watching holds a commercial break in the evening film.

He's feeling kind of happy with himself, he's patched things up with his wife and if he plays his cards right he could be sitting on the ugly sofa watching films like this every night.

The commercial ends before we've hit the motorway, but there's a news report, a short flash about some local crime and the stomach of Barbie's father rumbles.

He decides to ask his daughter if she or one of her two friends wants to go to the chip shop and because the news report is still running; he climbs the stairs to suggest the idea.

He's cautious about entering her bedroom and nearly changes his mind, he's not been the best father to her and he feels aware that he doesn't know the names of the two boys that rushed upstairs to see her.

He's even let a few noises slip past, turning the TV volume up each time.

You're only young once, he thinks.

He doesn't know it yet, but he's about to do the best thing a father can do for his child; he's about to save her life.

When he finds his daughter on the floor of her bedroom she's unconscious and he immediately calls the ambulance and then attempts to stop the bleeding. By this time Jack and I are miles away.

The police tell me she was brought to the hospital, this hospital.

They pause then, like kids do at the crucial point in a ghost story. I hide the concern I have about running into Barbie, what I might feel or do if I see her.

I ask them what film her dad was watching.

They don't like that. I mean they really don't like it.

They get up, brush bits of invisible dust off their uniforms and tell me not to worry, that Lucinda is safe and well and that I can finish my meal in peace; they're leaving now.

When they get up to go I ask them if the baby is okay, but they tell me no one knew anything about Barbie's pregnancy until I mentioned it and it's best if I don't try to discuss it with anyone else, or contact her, or go anywhere, or really even take a crap without permission, until they let me know otherwise.

X-RAY

There's a funeral, of course. It takes almost a month to release Jack's body and even now people are asking me the same questions.

Mostly they stick to stuff about what happened between the time we entered Barbie's house to the time Jack left his body in the Ford.

But others, officials mostly, want to concentrate on my blackouts.

It's February 28th 1998, and today is the day of the funeral. All I'm thinking about is how I have to face all the people I've hidden from over the last month.

School have been sending homework to me through the post, with a note that says it may help me keep my mind off things.

By *things* they mean the horrific death of my closest friend in the middle of our biggest crisis.

It's customary for a pupil to deliver homework to a classmate when they're sick or need to have a long time off school. With me I'm pretty sure no one wants to see me and that's why my homework keeps coming through the post.

The unopened letters are now growing mould under my bed where they are keeping a green tuna sandwich company.

Natasha hasn't spoken to me, when I call her house the phone just rings and rings and I picture her fat father, just sitting by the phone too tired to answer and Natasha in her room, refusing to give me another chance.

I've been spending all my time in my bedroom, and no one's stopping me.

I'm not even coming up to the living room for TV. But it's proving more and more difficult.

If Matka goes for a nap upstairs, there's no way she can hear me call from the basement and I won't get up and stand by the bottom of the steps leading up to her bedroom, so I just keep shouting until she happens to go to the living room or kitchen and hear my calls from the basement below.

Even then we spend a minute or two together and after she fetches me what I want she leaves again.

It's not that she doesn't care; it's how I like it now.

And because there's no one to say otherwise, I don't wash, I don't sleep and I only eat when Matka makes me.

I feel like I've shrunk back to a time before I knew Jack, like his death has caused every memory we've shared to evaporate.

I've gone back to wearing women's clothes all the time, which at the moment are mostly nightgowns and in an attempt to cheer me up Matka has even bought me a new wig. It looks exactly like my old hair looked.

Nobody from Jack's family have come to see me except Judy. She's been once a week and she'll be coming to pick me up today. Except it isn't really Judy, not the one I've known. She's completely clean now.

Her hair is fresh and styled, curly like Jack's but she's had it cut short so it's out of her eyes. Every time she sees me her skin is less sallow.

But the most amazing change about her are her eyes. She's sad that her brother is dead, she's completely cut up and it shows because now her eyes are able to show it. They're alive.

Jack is dead and Judy is alive. It must be tough for her parents, losing one child just as they get another back, but I bet they are glad flu season is finally over in their household.

On her last visit, nearly a week ago, I asked Judy if I could wear a dress to Jack's funeral and she said sure.

Matka lets me borrow a set of shoes she wore when she was still working. They're small, almost impossible to get into but I persist because I want to look right. Even though Jack wouldn't have given a shit, I need to let him and everyone else know I cared.

Matka helps me fit the wig, after I put on the dress and shoes. We stand in front of the mirror in the hall and she fusses over my outfit.

I wonder then if she would have liked a daughter instead.

She's never helped me dress like this before, only seen me this way drunk or stoned, but over the last month she's become accustomed to seeing her son sober and teary in nightgowns and now this must seem like the natural progression.

Besides, I'm up and I'm dressed.

A horn beeps outside and we're both startled. Matka rushes off upstairs and I stand in the hall, avoiding looking out the window because I know what will be there, I recognise the sound.

Matka comes back with her perfume and sprays it across my chest in a haze. Today she'll do anything to make me happy.

She opens the front door for me and Judy is waiting, dressed in a black suit, white shirt and black tie. It looks like we're going to a freak's prom.

'I thought we'd complement each other,' she tells me. I look at my dress, she's right. We make a good pair. Then she steps back and I see the Ford.

The bonnet and the side panels have been replaced, on one of them the blue seems slightly the wrong shade. But it's the Ford alright.

Matka makes a disapproving sound by breathing in through her nostrils. Judy, who once wouldn't have even noticed Matka was standing there, picks up on the noise and tells us it'll be therapeutic.

We don't have much choice because we've got a funeral to get to. I walk over to the passenger seat and wait for her to unlock the door.

She gets in and starts the engine. My first thought is that she's back on something but when I knock on the window she unlocks the door and explains it's been a long time since she drove this car. But before it was Jack's it was hers. *A lifetime ago*, she says. She's right.

I can't help looking for signs of blood, some evidence of Jack ever being here. The Ford is immaculate. Judy drives with the caution and control of a woman taking a car accident victim to the funeral of his friend. I tell her this and she thanks me.

Instinctively, I open the glove compartment for a tape, it's too quiet inside the car. Inside there aren't any tapes anymore, just an A-Z and a pamphlet about staying drug free.

'The car chewed up the tape.' Judy says 'That one of mine is still in there. The one from the crash.' We both look down at the slot. I push my finger inside and feel the edge of the tape.

'It's stuck alright.' I tell her.

'Is that your professional opinion?'

'Yeah.' I say, before touching it one last time.

184

'It works, you know. If you want to hear it.' She offers. 'I listen to it sometimes.'

I think about whether it's possible for the noises of the crash to be imprinted on the tape, if maybe even our thoughts have been projected onto that woman's voice.

I guess if that were true Judy would have mentioned it by now.

'Nah, it's fine.' I say 'I like the silence.'

The funeral is a bit of a farce. Half my school are here and although Judy guides me past them to sit with the family I can't help but get angry with all of them for using Jack's death as a good reason to skip class. They might as well have put a coach service on.

I can't see Barbie anywhere.

Jack's dad stands at the front of the church and unfolds a small scrap of paper. This close up I can see the sweat on his body. Then, as if he's heard me think this he takes a tissue from his trouser pocket and wipes his hands and face.

Judy leans over and tells me the suit he's wearing is the one he married her mother in. I don't know what to say to this so I just smile faintly. It's amazing how much time at funerals you end up trying to comfort others by giving them a vague smile. I'm sure an outsider would think we were all happy.

Jack's father reads a few words, while images of him flash on a projection screen.

'Jack was there when you needed him, he always had time for his grandparents. He was proud of his place in the family, he was my son.'

'He liked scuba-diving with his uncle and on weekends he would help out with DIY. His sister, Judy remembers him for his generosity – always taking her to dance classes in the car that she gave him. A car that was his pride and joy until the end.'

185

'His mother remembers how he liked making model aeroplanes in his bedroom as a child and I think we can all say we remember his good charity work. Although he didn't like to talk about it he helped out at the homeless shelter more than one Christmas.'

There's kind of a quiet moment of reflection, where the people listening are either nodding their heads and toasting Jack or wondering if they're at the right funeral.

Me, I'm in the second category. I'd try something along the lines of:

Jack always took the best pills at parties, he always reached the toilet if he was going to spew.

He was a proud of his bong collection and he wasn't going to give you a hard time about any issues. He was my best friend.

He liked committing petty crimes with me and on weekends he would get high in Barbie's attic.

His sister, Judy remembers him for his generosity – feeding her heroin addiction and not selling the car that she gave him. A car that was his pride and joy until the end –

That's as far as I get before the coffin is brought in. There's a tiny flower girl in front of it, maybe a cousin of Jack's or something.

I can't even look at the box that he's in, can't face being physically that close to him again. So instead, I look at the little girl. One of the laces of her little white trainers has come undone and I pray to - I pray to Jack that she won't fall over.

Outside, people stand around on the grass, waiting to walk over to bury the coffin. I look around the faces, searching but not really knowing who I'm looking for. Natasha, maybe. I realise I still haven't seen Barbie. Then I spot her, standing at the edge of a group of girls I don't know. I move closer and it takes her a second to see it's me.

'You're back on form then,' she says, indicating my dress. 'Like the night we met.' I look at the faces of the girls she is talking to. I don't recognise any of them.

Everything Barbie has said so far is for their benefit not mine. I want to ask where Natasha is but Barbie knows that and she isn't going to offer me any information. I want to ask if our baby is okay. If she thinks it might look like Jack.

I stand staring at her and when she realises I'm not going to leave she pulls me aside, grabbing my arm to navigate me to a quiet area. Looking at her I can see she's lost weight but I decide it won't do me any favours to tell her.

'I need to let you know, the baby is fine. It's only right you should hear that.' She cocks her head and thinks before she has to structure the next sentence so it can sound as adult as the last one.

'You also need to know, the baby isn't yours. It's Jack's. I'm almost sure of it.' Her lips tighten and she waits for my response. But I'm at my best friend's funeral and all I can feel now is a weird sense of hope that the baby really is his, then he can carry on in the form of a little baby with a cactus for a mother.

'You should speak to Judy,' I tell her 'She'd be really happy, I'm sure.'

Kids spill out onto the pathways of the cemetery. All around me adults are muttering about disrespect for the dead, the nameless dead. Here I am in a tight black dress and Matka's clerk shoes.

And by this point I haven't worn a piece of men's clothing for three weeks, I don't know if I ever will again.

When they lay the coffin down a small Wicca girl who I didn't even know knew Jack throws in some pentagram wood thing that she'd been waving like a wand all day, I want to strangle her. I think about doing this, my thumbs strong and calloused pushing on her ribbed windpipe as if it were an empty tampon tube.

But it's not just the girl because standing next to her, crowding around the open grave are tens of people just like her if not worse.

Within minutes, my anger just crumbles away, like I'm too hot and too tired to be so aggressive all the time anymore. Maybe it's the dress. Maybe it's death. Maybe I'm finally growing up.

People begin approaching the grave with handfuls of dirt and possessions.

Asides from his parents and Judy I don't think I know anyone else here. Who are all these people? Did Jack have some kind of secret life that I just never saw?

The more I think about it the more I am sure this must be the case.

The adults look rich, look normal, not the people Jack and I knew. They're more the people his family would be with. What kind of secret life is that? Then I realise, these people aren't part of his secret life. I am. To them I'm no different to the little Goth girls.

It's my turn to approach the grave and I haven't brought anything to leave with Jack so I fumble about in my handbag searching for something of significance to leave with him before he is covered with dirt. Then tangled between my hairbrush and the keys to my bike lock I feel one of his bead necklaces and for the first time today I start to cry.

Judy wanders over in a dazed state and holds my hand. Someone is making a speech and the weather is hot and sticky. I feel so young. Judy is possibly the oldest person I know – truly know. Here she is again taking responsibility for me on the day of her brother's funeral.

In a few hours we'll be laying in Jack's bedroom, and she'll hold me, just hold me, our skin on the freshly starched sheets he'll never sleep on while his wake continues downstairs without us. All the while I will recite like a golden mantra; *it's what he would have wanted.* I believe it's almost true.

When Judy sits up and decides it's time to go downstairs to be with the family, I skip the rest of the wake. It's mostly family here and it feels weird to be in Jack's house knowing he's not coming home.

Soon they'll pack up his bedroom and it'll be like they only have one child. At least they've got Judy back though; it almost seems like a fair trade.

She offers to drive me home, I accept because it feels like I've been walking home alone all my life.

In the car Judy tells me that shock is a strange thing, when someone dies unexpectedly - even someone nasty, they turn into a symbol of what they could have been at their full potential. In death they become a film star, a poet, a philosopher, a martyr, a hero, Ghandi. Although this may seem beautiful, you lose who they really were in the process. This change doesn't just happen to the jilted girlfriend or the proud father it happens to the tennis coach, the guy who walked to Italian class with them, the girl who served them lunch.

They all change the dead into their first true love. The dead become the most gifted loving person throughout time because they are no more.

She tells me it's our duty to remember everything about Jack, the good and the bad. That the most important thing to remember is that we loved him when he was alive, we loved him as the bastard he was not the saint he's become.

That's what matters.

She's scared we're going to lose him again, this time in our memories, she's scared I am the only one who saw him clearly when he was alive.

I want to tell her what Barbie said about the baby but it's been a long day and I'm tired. Let her have some good news tomorrow.

Despite it being the middle of the afternoon, all the curtains in the house are drawn. I walk through the empty living room, trying to make sense of the shapes the furniture make in the half light and nearly trip over a heavy metal object. I lean down to get a look at it and it's Papa's toolkit.

I stand very still, feeling like a mouse in a shoebox. He could be in this room right now. I breathe in deeply, like it'll help me tell if Papa is in the house or not. I'm stuck and I know it. I can't stand in the dark for hours waiting for someone to find me and so I walk as purposefully as I can through the living room, then the kitchen and finally into my bedroom.

All the clean clothes on my bed are male and when I look through them I see they don't belong to me at all, they belong to Charles. Is Matka giving me Papa's clothes?

I shed the black dress and let it sit in a crumple on the floor.

My back is moist from sweating and the damp air of my bedroom.

Slowly, I pick up a t-shirt of Papa's and slide it over my head. It feels cool, smells fresh and isn't actually that large. There are some trousers too. The length is fine, but the waist band is way too big, so I search around in a draw for my school belt and loop it through. It has a weird kind of feel, bunching up around my waist, but I like it. I add some shoes of my own from under my bed and that's when I look at the box with the gun in. I can't bring myself to open the box, so I draw myself as close to the bed as I can and slide an arm under, with my hand reaching inside the case.

The thick plastic covers of a porn magazine meet my fingers, then the gun, feeling like it's made of marble it's so cool. Safe, it's remained perfectly preserved wrapped around a pair of fake silk pants belonging to a girl too stupid to lock her locker.

I was going to just take my hand out, get on with whatever I was doing but all I can think about is the gun. It's like my arm is stuck under the bed and won't be released until I take a look at the weapon.

I pull the gun out. It's heavier than I remembered. I want to open the barrel, look at the bullets, but I don't know how. I wonder what they look like, if they're shiny or matt. It's hard to imagine something so small could kill you just because it's going so fast.

I take a go at moving round the room, holding the gun up at chest height in Papa's clothing. I aim at things; a book, a cuddly toy, the stencils on the wall, then specifically, the heart stencil.

'Bang,' I say out loud to no one in particular.

Five seconds later there really is a bang, well more of a crash coming from upstairs. I rush up to the kitchen, then realising I've still got the gun in my hand, tuck it into one of the deep pockets of Papa's trousers.

There's still no one downstairs.

I stand in the shadows of the lounge, wondering whether to open the curtains or not when the noise comes again. No, this is a different noise, more of a screech, except it doesn't even sound human.

It's coming from upstairs.

I stand in the dark at the foot of the stairs, steadying myself. I crane my head forward, trying to hear what might be going on.

If Matka is having a nap, would she be pleased enough to see me in these clothes that she wouldn't be angry about being woken up? Before I can decide, another noise, this time a shriek, drives me up the stairs and toward my parent's bedroom.

When I get there the door is closed. I don't know what I was expecting and I've no idea whether this is normal or not, but it's stunted my plan. There's no key hole to look through, there's just a closed wooden door.

191

I could creep back down the steps now, go and sit in my room and have a very different life. I don't. I stay outside the door, pressing my ear to the wood just like I did the night of my party when Barbie was in there with some guy.

I'll just wait for the noises to return.

I try and think of the last time I did this but I've not been upstairs when my parents are home for way over two years, I'm not even sure what happened the last time I was here when I wasn't supposed to be.

It takes five, nearly six minutes, but the sounds come back. I don't have my Casio on, so I can't tell exactly how long it is, but it's long enough to let me know something is up. The noises start quietly at first, the kind of thing you could attribute to a bad dream or a case of cramp, but then they get louder. I am sure it's Matka.

When I can't stand the sounds anymore I put my hand on the doorknob and turn it slowly. The catch releases inside and I push the door open a crack then let go.

The door drifts open an inch, then another. But it just doesn't stop and then, soon I am standing in the doorway of my parent's bedroom with the door hanging wide open.

What happens next is confusing. Matka is in bed, but instead of looking tired and weary, or angry that I've broken the house rules and woke her up, she looks alive and very much awake. She's naked and there's a man with her and when they see me, or sense that I'm there, they move quickly, covering themselves with sheets and blankets.

I know I should look down but I can't and when I don't make any sign that I'm going to move, Matka says something to the man and the man turns and it's Charles.

He looks at me and because I've broken the rules or because I'm in his clothes or because he's just mad he starts shouting and because I'm stressed and confused I shout back. I feel like I've just caught them having an affair and I actually say this several times while we're all shouting but no one hears it.

Matka gets up with a sheet wrapped around her body and starts moving toward me. At first I think she's coming in for a hug but she's actually trying to shoo me downstairs and shut the door. Like what I've seen is going to disappear if she puts a bit of wood between me and him.

I keep asking Matka again and again to tell me what is going on, what Charles is doing in our house. She replies for me to wait downstairs and she'll follow me, but I know she won't. I don't move. I make a point of not even moving a muscle. Papa's trousers are bunched around my waist and I just want to yank off my belt and hit him with it, but I know for her sake I can't do anything like that.

I watch Matka, one of her hands is wrapped around the edge of the sheet and I focus on her balling up the material, wringing it in anticipation, or fear, of what will happen next.

When she sees I'm not moving, she tries again.

'Please Charlie, just wait downstairs.'

'Can you explain this?' I ask gesturing wildly about the room. She considers this for a moment and then asks me what is it I want to know.

'This,' I shout. I don't want to have to say the words and I think she should realise that. She looks around the room, puzzled. Trying to see what I see.

'Him.' I point at my dad. 'What is he doing here?'

'Your father?' How the woman can sound so incredulous I just don't know.

'Yes.'

She looks at him and there's some kind of silent agreement between them. I swear her eyes look sad. She goes to open her mouth but before she can Charles speaks.

'I live here Charlie, where else would I be?'

The world shifts.

A thick gush of vomit rises from the pit of my stomach and surfs across my mouth, onto the floor. I step back to stop it splashing on me. It's just a small bit, but I can't help looking at it, a tiny pool of sick sitting on the top of the carpet. Spittle hangs in long strings from my mouth. I'm a fucking Saint Bernard.

My eyes are blurring, I don't know if its tears or shock, but the puddle of vomit is swimming in and out of focus. I remember my doctor once saying that if I ever got in a situation beyond my control to take three deep breaths and reassess, so I try.

Neither of them are saying anything, they're just waiting for me. So when my three deep breaths are up, I lift my head to look at them - my parents, together in bed.

I half expect Charles to be gone, to disappear, to be erased. That's what normally happens, after all.

He's there. Looking larger than life. I test the water.

'You've never left?' I ask.

'God, Charlie, yes. 'Papa is impatient already, like we do this every afternoon.

'The three of us live here,' Matka pitches in.

'I've been blocking you out,' I tell him. I'm almost ready to meet his eye but not quite.

'You hide,' he says.

'We knew something like this might happen,' Matka says. 'Now let's deal with it.'

And I want to ask was she thinking of her only child going insane as *something like this*. Charles eyes me up. For the first time I eye him back. Is it me shutting out my memories? Am I just refusing to accept the parts of my life I don't want? If that's true, why aren't I a Virgin again, why isn't Jack alive?

'You only see what you want to,' Charles tells me. It's then that something inside me snaps, not like the way a twig snaps, more like somewhere in my brain a little switch has been triggered and now the world is a different place.

Things start falling into position then, first slowly, then faster, like memories and signs are literally dropping from the sky. I look up to catch them, hands spread open.

'The boy has gone cuckoo,' Charles says an invisible audience. But he's wrong, it's the opposite.

I am seeing clearly. So fucking clearly it makes my eyes burn.

Matka guides me to the edge of her bed, *their bed*, and the three of us talk about all the evidence my brain chooses to suppress along with the knowledge that Papa lives with me.

So much makes sense now; how Matka always lays three plates at dinner time, how Charles' tool kit is always lying around the house. How I had to finish my birthday party by four because the only time Charles and I ever see each other is in the early hours of the morning when he's finishing work.

Or now, in the early afternoon before he leaves.

This is why his clothes are always being washed and hung up around the house. That one makes me look down at his clothes, his clothes that I have got on while he is in bed, naked.

I pull at the t-shirt I'm wearing, try to take it off but for some reason I can't.

I have to get away from Papa, it's too dangerous. And he's been here all along. The smell of him creeps up through my nostrils and I know I can't get it out of my lungs.

It's suffocating me.

Matka leans in toward me, her arms curls around my shoulder and the sheet she's wrapped in begins to slip. 'It's okay, Charlie. It's okay,' she says trying to make me move toward her, to come in for an embrace.

'Don't pamper him.' Papa's voice is thick with anger but there's something else about it. It's got that everyday element to it, it sounds familiar. It sounds almost boring.

All the times we've spoken recently, all the times I can remember I would be scared by now, but at this moment I feel nothing. I mean what have I got to lose? If he does this to me every day and I'm still here it can't be as bad as I make out, can it?

To stop Matka moving any closer to me Charles lifts himself out of bed.

The covers shielding him fall and he's completely naked. He doesn't need to hide behind sheets. I suddenly want to get out of his clothes more than ever and some part of my brain, trying to rationalise things tells me all he wants from me is his clothes back then he'll leave me alone. Could that be it?

I get up and tear at the trousers, but this time, not in fear to remove his stink but in the hope that I don't need them, that if I give them back he'll leave me alone. He stops moving toward me when he sees me yanking the material, they both do.

I guess I look pretty crazy, but it has to be done. I don't know what other option I have but to give in. I'm still pulling at his clothes when the gun falls out my pocket.

I've heard that when a person experiences a large shock, like finding out reality isn't what they thought it was, their behaviour becomes erratic. I can now confirm this to be true.

All eyes are on the gun and it's during these moments that I try and put together some kind of plan B. I'm not thinking straight, it's like I'm in the kind of sick dream I'd make up to keep my doctor amused.

There's a gun on the floor of my parent's bedroom, they're both naked and I'm dressed in Papa's clothes.

I lift my eyes from the gun and onto Charles, he's still looking at it, and for the first time there's an emotion other than anger registering on his face. If this was a different time or place I think I'd smile at having shocked Papa, but right now I just want this to end.

I start thinking that if Charles has never left, maybe he should now.

I've got used to a life without him, a home without him. I start to reason that he's dangerous and that when this is over he's going to be mad, perhaps worse than I've ever seen him before.

Somehow this idea grow and grows in my head until I get to thinking that if I don't fight my way out of this one then there's a chance he could harm both of us, he could even kill us now I've put a weapon in the room.

This is what I say to myself as we're all looking at the gun.

I stop thinking about if I should get the gun and start trying to work out whether to edge down and pick it up or grab it.

In the end I don't have to decide.

'Don't worry about the gun,' I tell my parents. The three of us are surrounding the gun, with bent knees, like we're about to pounce.

'Really, it's fine,' I say. To show I mean it I put my hands flat out in front of me in what I think is the least gun grabbing position I can think of.

By this moment we've all already made our decisions on how to deal with the situation and everything settles into place. Our fate has been written for us and there's no point fighting against it.

Charles, knowing he isn't going to be able to get to the gun before I do, decides that he still rules in this house whether his son is having a nervous breakdown or not.

He shouts at me to step away from the gun, to wait downstairs and he will come and deal with me in his own good time.

I'm pretty sure he'll be dealing with Matka first. But I'm not going to go back down stairs now I've finally made it up here. I'm going to face things from now on.

I'd like to think it's something cruel Papa says to me that makes Matka realise just how good a life without him would be, or maybe it's the ideal of living the reality I live in where he's already gone, but while Charles threatens me, Matka moves closer and closer until she very calmly bends down and picks up the gun.

Very slowly, Papa's head moves to turn and face Matka. It's like watching *The Exorcist* as his head rotates on his neck and his eyes open wider and wider, transmitting his disbelief for everyone in a ten foot radius to read.

I silently pray to anyone who might be listening that she just turns and shoots him now. I am sure she'd get away with it, after all those years of abuse.

We could bury him under the scrap of grass by my bedroom window, or if we were caught I'd take the blame. I want to let her know I'd do that for her.

Because she can't shoot her husband, she does the next best thing. She hands the gun to me. Our hands touch for a second, maybe two and I want to look at her but I'm angry and scared and I want to know why she never told me the truth about Charles. She obviously knew.

Charles moves toward me, circling two slow steps at a time with his arms held out the way a man might prepare to wrestle a bear. He launches himself at me, but I see it coming. I always see it coming, I just don't react.

Today is different for many reasons and this is one of them; when he comes at me I move to the side, just a quick, light step and as he dives he catches the side of my body.

I didn't move far away enough, and both of us end up crashing onto the bed.

He lands on top of me and the fall makes him let out this comical *oouff!!* noise.

I try to move, to get my balance back but he's much heavier than I imagined and it feels like all the air is being pushed out of my lungs by weight alone.

We're struggling, or more I'm struggling and he's pinning me down. The gun is still in my hand but it's wedged along with me somewhere under his flesh.

I'm struggling and I know he's waiting for me to wear myself out, I've seen him do the same thing to Matka. But then his weight seems to double and he slumps forward onto me.

Matka has hit him with something, but it only stuns him for a moment. Later I find out it's the Bible, his Bible at that. I never even knew he read it.

Charles leans off me and pushes Matka away. I take a huge gasp of air and I hear her fall on the floor and get up again. With Charles still on me all I can see is the ceiling and the corner of the room.

He turns his attention back to me and this time when she strikes him I'm ready. I relax my body as much as I can and he rolls into me with so much force he turns over, so now I am on top of him.

There's a look of bewilderment on his face and I see that he's not looking at me, he's looking at the gun I've still got clutched in my hand.

In my head I pull the trigger of the gun and wait. His body stiffens beneath me and it's only when I see the spread of blood behind his right shoulder I realise I've shot him. Maybe he wheezes like a fish that's been taken out of water.

Maybe some rosy coloured spit comes out of his mouth. Matka rejoices and we're free.

But I can't do that. I can't shoot him.

'Can you die from being shot in the chest?' I ask Matka. She's standing somewhere behind me, not daring to move any closer.

She doesn't say anything and I can picture her clutching the book, like she clutches everything else. When this is over I want her to hold me like that.

I trace the barrel of the gun over Papa's bare chest. I want to see his breathing get faster, to see him face the idea of dying. I want him to reconsider why he didn't deal with my blackouts sooner.

I don't like being the one who doesn't get let in on the joke. I don't like it even more when I don't get let in on real life.

'Can you die from being shot in the chest?' I ask Matka again, partly in the hope that she'll just let me know she's still in the room.

'Of course you can, you bloody idiot,' Charles says. 'Haven't I taught you better than that?'

And even now his voice is controlling me, while I'm on top of him, fully clothed with a gun in my hand he's the one that's calling the shots.

But there's something there, in his voice, just a hint of a tremor, almost undetectable but enough to drive me on.

I let the barrel of the gun skid slowly up his chest until it's resting in the little V shape of his collar bone. I want him to sweat, to get so nervous he has to swallow so I can see his Adam's apple bob up and down above the gun.

This is it, I am going to kill my own father.
I lift my weight up on my knees so I'm not touching any part of his body, I don't want to be touching him when I pull the trigger in case there's some kind of spasm or I misfire.

'Stand back,' I shout to where I think Matka will be in the room. It sounds like I'm setting off fireworks. I guess I am.

I'm ready for the blood splatter, for the coughing and the choking, him thrashing about like a fish pulled out of the sea.

I cock the safety and I hear Matka take a deep breath. Is a Bible about to come crashing down on my head too?

To his credit, Charles still has his eyes open. I don't know if he'll keep them open at the end as I'm about to close mine. I keep expecting him to come out with some speech, maybe tell me off for closing my eyes, killing him in a cowardly way.

It doesn't happen like that. Matka doesn't appear to be stopping me and neither does Charles. Then it comes.

'Son?' he says 'You don't want to do this.' It isn't a command, just the softly spoken words of a father to his child.

He's right, I don't. Not because I don't want him dead and gone but I don't know where my life will go if I do shoot him.

I look at his face and it's covered in tiny, tiny lines. He looks old.

'Just put the gun down,' he says. 'Everything will be fine.' And I want to believe him, I desperately want to and suddenly I feel so tired, not just of these events but of my whole life. I wish I could just lie down, just put my head on his chest right here and fall asleep forever.

I rest the gun flat on his chest; it isn't cold anymore.

I know by doing this I'm giving in, to everything. To Charles, to the blackouts, to Matka's constant fear and unhappiness.

I just want to stop. This morning Jack was buried. Was that really only a few hours ago?

I lift myself off Charles and stand next to Matka in the corner of the room, slowly bending my legs where they've lost the flow of circulation. I've no idea how long Papa and I were stuck in that position together. My hand is still stiff and cramped from clutching to the gun for so long.

This action of opening and closing my hand is what makes me realise that I've left the gun unattended. Matka and I look at each other, and I think she's made the same connection as I have, but that's not it. She's trying to tell me that Charles is standing behind me, and this time he is holding the gun.

By now, this is the third time I've had this very gun pointed at me, but this is the first time I've ever been truly scared it could end in death.

I'd like to say I dropped to my knees in some kind of submission, but really my legs gave way beneath me and it was Charles who pulled me back up into a kneeling position.

'Do you want to die, is that it.' And even though it's phrased like a question, I know Charles doesn't mean it as one.

He's telling me I'm stupid for leaving the gun with him, that when his voice changed before it was all bullshit and if I fell for it I am all the more stupid.

I don't answer.

Because I am tired now, I want to give in. I'm ready to end it. Part of me still thinks I left the gun with him to get myself in this impossible situation, because let's face it, Matka was right all along; I am my own worst enemy.

There's another part of me, a much smaller part that is beginning to accept that sometimes I just do things, however stupid because I can't face up to the real world. So I put myself somewhere else instead.

That's what I'm doing now.

I close my eyes. I'm at the back of my house and the wind is rushing through my t-shirt. I've fallen asleep in maths class and Natasha is nudging me awake. I'm at a party, surrounded by kids dancing and bumping into me.

It's not working, I'm still here. The blackouts won't come now I know the truth. Papa is shaking me, trying to get me to open my eyes. I keep them scrunched shut and wait to see if he'll prize them open.

I know all Matka can do is stand in the corner and worry. I've got no chance of another surprise attack from her, I'm on my own. It's not her fault, she's been dealing with Charles in her own way for years, I guess we both have.

These are my last few minutes and I know it.

On the floor of my parent's bedroom, curled into a ball I realise the following three things:

First, Jack died the most frustrating and unromantic death of the century and I am going to outlive him by just over a month.

Then, it occurs to me that there's a tiny chance I could be a father, but no one will ever be able to tell if Barbie's child is mine or Jack's or someone else's altogether because we'll both be dead.

I'm pretty much okay with this because I could have been a rapist and I wasn't, I could have been a murderer and I'm not, and now I could be a father and I'll never get to know, but neither will the rest of the world.

It will give people something to talk about.

I said there were three things. The final one is the only one I really have a problem with, because now I know Papa is going to kill me, I realise I am never going to get Natasha back.

'I don't want to die,' I say and Papa pulls the trigger.

PAPA

It's not like I imagined, this place. Before I got here I thought it was going to be wall-to-wall whitewash, and electric shock therapy, but it turns out I couldn't have been more wrong.

There are no straps, or shocks and hardly anything is white. Instead, there are family counselling sessions, stress bags and colours everywhere, enough to blind you, almost.

That gets to me, like all the people whose purpose in life it is to stay here and get better are being helped by the bright red tables and plastic yellow flowers on top of them.

Despite this, I actually like it in the hospital.

It has this safety net, invisible, but I can feel it all the time. It's made up of the nurses and doctors who talk to Matka in hushed tones, who will chat with you about anything for as long as you want but always have their radars tuned in for some trouble growing among the patients.

The safety net is made up of the men who mop the floors, eyes down, ears open, waiting to report back any signs of trouble and sometimes signs of hope.

Most of all it's made up of the visitors. Families and friends who struggle through rush hour traffic after long painful days at the office, or the factory to see their loved ones, most of them not knowing who they will meet when they get there because the people they love aren't always people anymore.

When Papa shot me, the moment before his finger squeezed the trigger I realised that I wanted to live. Even in a world that contained Charles and one that didn't have Jack in it.

Even in a world where I hide from the truth.

Charles pulls the trigger and I catch my breath, a real sucker-punch feeling that leaves me fighting to get a lungful of air and the next thing I know I'm bathing in this warm wet glow and I'm wondering if this is really how it feels to die, there's no pain, just a dizzy sensation.

My eyes are screwed shut and I'm just waiting for the pain to hit and get the final blackout, the one I don't wake up from. But it doesn't come.

The warmth that I thought was my blood wasn't blood at all, it was urine. Charles pulls the trigger and the panic induces a breathing fit, the fear that's climbing up my throat makes me piss myself. Hardly heroic, I know.

Charles pulls the trigger, but there are no bullets. It looks like there never were. I should really check these things.

Today, it's sunny; not that cold white sunlight that you get in winter, but the real, buttery yellow stuff that slips over you and warms your skin until you realise it's pretty good to be alive, wherever you are, whatever you're doing, whatever you've done.

And I'm seeing Papa today, it's been a month since our last visit together and we sit in the ward, him sprawled in an armchair, me on a stool, my elbows tucked into my crotch like an autistic kid.

He tells me my hair is getting longer, and I run my fingers through it, it's a couple of inches now, nearly long enough to hide the scar that runs across my skull.

He told me once it looked like someone had stuck a knife in my head and tried to peel it like an orange. Only it turned out I was too tough, more like a walnut. That's the closest he's got to complimenting me in my life and I treasure it, running the words over again and again in the dark at night.

I'm thinking about asking if I can get it shaved again. I like the drama that comes with a scar, the way you can see people trying to work out how it came to be on my head.

Of course, everyone expects some horror story, but I don't tell it often. Get over it or let it kill you, right?

Charles is mellow, as if since the accident, by which I mean since he tried to kill his son, life has slowed down or he's been forced to slow with it. It's hard to tell through the drugs and it doesn't really matter how it happened, just that it did.

Some days I wonder if he'd have been slower with a bullet in his body. Some days I wonder if I would.

The people that know what happened, which aren't many, sometimes ask me how I can spend time with him, even in a safe environment like the hospital.

I've learnt now, and I keep learning, that he's part of my life and he's part of me. I can't shut him out whatever he does. We are both learning to be together. That's the only way I am going to get better.

He offers me a crossword clue and I know he hasn't thought about whether I'll have a chance of knowing it, but somehow that makes it more special. He's not manipulating, he's just trying to share something with me in any way he can.

It's about photosynthesis, the clue. One of us suggests asking a nurse for the dog-eared copy of the thesaurus but neither of us goes to move.

I let the sun hit my bare arms and soothe the tension in my muscles. I'm wearing a vest and a pair of tracksuit bottoms, it's been a long time since I wore women's clothes but when I dream I still dream in dresses.

If I focus my mind hard, I can make it travel into the house, down the steps to the dark basement where the most harmless thing packed under the bed are suitcases and suitcases of girl's clothes, all in my size. They'll be growing musty down there, but that's where they are staying, for a while anyway.

There were some conditions after the accident. Not all of them I agreed to at first, but I soon realised I wasn't able to bargain for anything. I just had to suck it all in and nod, something I am still getting used to.

The first condition, set by Matka of all people, was that the girl's clothes went away, at least until I was sixteen. If my hair hadn't been shorn by Charles, or later the paramedics at the crash, I think she'd have asked for me to lose that too. I'm pretty sure that wouldn't have come into it if she hadn't helped me get dressed the day of Jack's funeral, the day with the gun.

I felt at first like she wanted a new son in place of the abused little fuck up, but she kept telling me she just wanted to have a break from me, that's what this time is all about. Everybody getting a break from me.

The second condition was that I didn't have any kind of physical or sexual relationship with anyone. It would be pretty hard to do even if I wanted to, there's no opportunity and there's no one that wants me.

Except, every now and then one of those men with mops will look up from where his eyes rest on the shiny tiles and wink at me. I know then, I just know he's thinking about screwing me. It's not as bad as it seems, it's all over in a matter of minutes.

The final condition was Barbie. We're not to see each other; no contact at all, no visits, no phone calls, at least until the baby is born.

I've heard of this kind of thing when kids kill someone or something and it's considered too dangerous for them to be together because it's too intense.

That's not it with us, that's not it at all.

I should point out first that I do blame her for Jack's death and most days I say this to the people that know what happened.

I don't blame her in an angry grief way and not in an angst-ridden teen way either. It's her fault. Simple. It's mine too. And that is the thing that keeps us tied, like an invisible thread he's wound around both our wrists.

Some kind of practical joke from beyond the grave.

We're kept apart because people, I mean people like my doctor and her mother, those people, think that if I got my hands on her I'd punish her, or I'd use that invisible thread to choke her. I used to think the same thing, but it's not true.

It's not just because of the baby either. The baby that didn't exist anywhere but her head for the longest time and now, according to Judy, is starting to show.

It's because I know how much it hurts to lose someone. I'm not giving that pain to anyone; I am just going to sit here holding my own little piece of burning coal.

It's weird but in losing Jack I have gained a new place in the world, I've been something real to worry about and I've had something real to worry about and I've found I don't like either of them.

So you can cut off the *Samaritans*, cut off *Child Line*, because when it comes to it, there is nothing in the world but me and all the people I will ever meet and the hope that maybe we can get along without killing each other.

Papa gives me another crossword clue and I look up from where I've been staring at the highly polished floor.

It's supposed to be an easy one but neither of us know the word that should be filled in the little white squares.

He flings the paper down, the muscles in his arm jumping to the surface, a little reminder from his body of who he was. But his eyes are calm and he sweeps the paper up and starts to read the cartoons on the back page.

These visits, these rare visits with him, mostly consist of us sitting together, me staring into nothing like a junior space cadet and him reading the paper or some old journal that's lying around.

Once I found him reading a *Woman's Weekly* but he hid it under his chair when he saw the nurse guide me down the corridor to meet him.

At the other end of the hall is the clock that says when visiting time is over. It looks just like one of those cheap white school clocks but instead of telling the time, it just moves in and out of visiting hours.

One of the nurses told me that it's important to remember while we're here we don't think about the outside world and just focus on what's happening here, now.

It's useless to me because with the way we're positioned my back is facing the clock and if I turn around then Charles will think I'm waiting for the session to end.

Which I'm not, I just like to know times and dates and things.

I rub my arm where my Casio was.

I haven't seen my watch since the day he tried to shoot me.

Even now my life is still very much controlled by time, like the days that turn to months that bring Barbie more weight in the shape of a baby inside her.

There'll be tests when it's born, and I'll have to give some blood and answer some questions.

Every day I pray that it's mine and every day I pray that it's Jack's, like somehow part of him will be back in the world again.

There are more options than that. If it's not mine, we won't know it's Jack's; there's no affordable way of testing.

We can't demand that Barbie get paternity tests from every boy that came within a foot of her around Christmas.

I still believe there was someone with her at my party and if I'd learned to open my parent's bedroom door earlier maybe I could have warned him.

Whoever the father is, the baby is coming and we're all facing it.

In a way the kid already has three families, with mine, Barbie's and Jack's all preparing to welcome him.

And whether he was created in my parent's bedroom with some random kid, or with me in the basement or if he's the last shred of a dead lover, he's still connected to me and although I'm not ready for him I'm ready to accept him.

That's another thing, I've only told Judy but I'm sure the baby is a boy. It'll be a tough life ahead of him if he is, a lot of rejection and maybe a problem with roll models but that's what happens when you've got a cross-dressing fuck-up for a father, or a dead stoner. He'll be okay, and if he's not he'll be strong, even with a cactus for a mother.

Judy talks to Barbie most days, and visits her a lot with gifts and books on how to look after children.

I know part of her is nursing Barbie because she believes that her dead brother's memory is being carried in Barbie's septic tank of a womb, but now it's more than that, they've bonded in that weird, complete way only girls seem to be able to do.

That bond that I wanted for such a long time, with anyone really, just doesn't seem available to males. Even ones in dresses.

So I've lost a lot of people in a lot of different ways; Jack is dead, Barbie is off limits and I've not seen Natasha and doubt I ever will.

Maybe that will change sometime in the future and if it does I'd welcome her but I don't want to wait for too long.

Soon someone else will find her, someone who can give her what she's looking for and then that boy will soil her and she won't be the little naked blonde that was my fifteenth birthday present anymore.

Even then I'd still ask for her back.

Through all the people I've lost, I've gained a father. He's here whether I like it or not and very slowly, with or without the drugs, I think we're going to start liking each other one day.

Matka says I'll understand it better when I'm a father myself, so that'll be in about four months.

When the visiting session ends Charles and I both stand up and move our arms like we're geese trying to get into the sky.

He steps forward first and wraps his heavy arms around my shoulders. He connects for the shortest time possible but it's enough.

The sessions here have taught me to read when he's saying he loves me. Now I just need him to start liking me.

Starchy nurses appear from every corner and there's one for each patient. A strict brunette with bright red lips comes to escort me off and Papa brushes down his coat while I get ready.

As we walk off he asks if I've ever read some book about cuckoos and when I say no he promises to try and find a copy for me.

We walk down long corridors and my nurse guides me past wards full of screaming patients, sleeping patients, dead ones and ultra-thin ones until we reach the double doors at the end of the hall. She doesn't say anything to me the whole time we are walking. She doesn't even look at me until we nod goodbye and I push the doors.

There's a little guy in a tiny room made of reinforced glass, the kind that has chicken wire inside it and when he sees me he presses one of the buzzers on his desk, the double doors open and I walk through.

The sun is even stronger outside and I can barely see Judy leaning against the Ford.

I shield my eyes from the sun and Judy calls that we have to be fast because she thinks she's parked where the ambulances go.

I didn't think this kind of place had ambulances and she reminds me how not all patients sign themselves into the hospital as willingly as Papa did.

We get in the Ford and the cracked imitation leather scorches my legs through my tracksuit bottoms. Judy tells me she has something for me, it's in the glove compartment.

My head fills up with images of bits of Jack's corpse but I close my eyes and count to ten, just like the doctors tell you to. Papa may be the one in the institution but most days I figure I need just as much help as he does.

My hand reaches out to the glove box, and I wonder if Judy can see it shaking, but when I look over she's busy watching the road.

The inside of the glove box is dark, so I have to reach in to see what this thing might be. The fact that there are no reggae tapes in there makes a lump come up in my throat, but it passes as quickly as it arrived.

I pull out the object and it's my Casio. I know it can't have been here all along and Judy explains that it must have come off when we were in Jack's room at the wake.

I know this probably means that they're packing his room away now and when I look at her, her expression confirms this.

'It's what we all need,' she tells me.

I shrug, and look down at the Casio so she won't be able to tell that the lump is back.

The safe little numbers are still turning and I stare for a long time at the date, the time, and the seconds passing from one moment of my life to another, reminding me that things change.

It's May 16th 1998 and I'm riding around in a blue Ford Cortina with my best friend's sister. The girl who is driving is going to change my life, but if I want her to I've got to do start changing things myself.

I take off the Casio and I tell myself it's not 10:28, May 16th 1998. It's just another Saturday.

AFTERWORD

I wrote this book when I was 23. Reading it over now, I'm occasionally self-conscious about the quality of the writing but I still care for the characters, especially when they behave like idiots.

That's probably because they are me, or were me at one point in my life. Except maybe Barbie; she's just a bitch.

Now I'm a bit older, I might not feel their angst as much as I once did, but I do love them for their resilience, their petulance and their bravado.

What can I say? I was young and I needed the experience.

ABOUT THE AUTHOR

Kimber Cross wanted to be a gymnast, a mechanic and a gynecologist. Instead, she became a writer.

She lives in London.

You can find her at mskimbercross.tumblr.com or you can email her at mskimbercross@gmail.com.

PLAY: Not Safe For Work

A novel

By Kimber Cross

It's the end of the nineties. Lauren is measuring her life out in lines of coke when the call comes: the man who destroyed her life is back.

Now she's got a reason to live, at least for long enough to bring him down, but she's just a few grams away from a trip to the morgue.

PLAY: Not Safe For Work
An extract

LAUREN

I'm submerged in a tub that's filled to the brim with
the hottest water I can bear and while I'm under, scalding
my sins away, I hear the phone ring.
I burst up, sending waves crashing over the side and
soaking the floor. When I try to get out, chase the sound
of the phone to the living room, my body betrays me. I
seize up, unable to bend my knees and curl my hips up out
of the water.
There are people it would be best if I didn't talk to. I wish
I'd worked that out before giving them my phone number.
     I stay hunched in the tub, my knees tucked under my
chin, an imagined emergency position for bath-time
disasters. Drops of water cling to my skin as it puckers and
turns cold. I realise I'm holding my breath.
     The phone keeps ringing.
     I picture the living room, lights off and perfectly still
except for the plastic phone screwed to the wall, dancing
in its cradle. My palms begin to prickle, as if my skin is
anticipating contact with the receiver.
     The sound is maddening. I slap my hands over my
ears just as the answer phone clicks into place. I wait.
There's static, then my own voice sounding coked up and
frantic. I'm telling the hordes of callers that I'm out at a
party or just too busy to come to the phone.
     My message is followed by a beep and then as I strain
to hear more, suspecting that my mystery caller has hung
up, there comes a sound I recognise instantly; a single sigh,
deep from my mother's chest and into the phone, where it
will remain trapped in my answer-machine. Just as I think
that's it, her entire message - a sigh to sum up her eternal

disappointment and the months of silence between us -
she starts to talk.

'He's back,' she says, 'the boy.' She knows his name,
just doesn't want to say it. That's fine. I don't want to hear
it. We both know who she's talking about.

I picture her standing in the hall of our family home,
curling and uncurling the telephone cord in her fat fingers.
She sounds old and tired, 'I just thought you should know,
Lauren.'

She says my name like it's exotic to her, even though
she was the one to give it to me. She probably hasn't
spoken my name since I left.

There's another pause and I wonder if she knows I'm
in, and she's just hanging on the other end of the line until
I relent and pick up. I sink back into the bath, the hot
water forming a protective seal around my skin.

'Come home, Lauren,' my mother tells the answer
phone. 'I think it's time you come home and sort this
mess out.'

DAVID

The curtains aren't even drawn yet and she's taking
off her uniform. The starch in my shirt itches at the back
of my neck and I want to peel off too. Trouble is, if I do, I
don't know how she'll react. She's weird like that, Mandy.

You think you've got her squared and then she freaks
out over nothing and hits you with a coffee tray.

We're in one of the posh suites, right on the top
floor. She's supposed to be servicing this room and for
some reason she's decided she wants to service me instead.

I'm not going to complain, but my break ends in
twelve minutes and if I'm not back on front desk, there'll
be hell from the management. I need this job, probably
more than I need to get laid.

I'm standing in the middle of the room, waiting to see which way it's going to go, when she pulls off her pinafore. It's peach-coloured, doesn't do anything for her bleached hair and pale skin. It's not a sexy lacy thing either, not like what you see maids wear in pornos. It's just a giant rectangle with a big O in the middle for her head to go through. I'm glad it's off. I don't know if I could follow through with the sex otherwise.

She starts to undo her dress, but it's taking too long. All those buttons. I don't want to scare her off by rushing things and pulling my pants down or anything. I just stand there, gawping at her. She looks up and gives me this massive dirty smile. Mouth full of metal – she still has her braces at nineteen.

Looks like they would hurt – me, not her. I mentally draw a line through *blowjob* as an option with Mandy. Still, she's smiling so I smile back, hands in my pockets, waiting for a sign to go ahead and get things started. She kicks her heels off, dances around them a bit. I loosen my red polyester tie. Just to keep my hands busy. It's getting more complicated than one of those animal sex rituals you see on *The Discovery Channel*.

I can just hear some posh git narrating the whole thing: *here we have the mating ritual of the average hotel worker. Note that the male has absolutely no balls.*

Mandy pulls her tights down and they stretch as she tugs them away from her feet. They're tan, like the colour of chicken gravy. Her legs underneath are greyish white. I take off my waistcoat, unlace my shoes. I feel like I'm making a big commitment by taking these shoes off. This might just happen.

Eleven minutes 'til shift starts.

I undo the cuffs of my shirt and roll up my sleeves. She must think I'm getting ready to do the washing up, not have sex with her.

It doesn't help that we've been here maybe three or four times since I started this job and every one of those times she's backed out. She won't explain why and I've already learned that you've just got to take what you're given with Mandy.

I move over to close the curtains, clocking the time on the way. She likes it like that, with the curtains closed, I know that much. Makes her feel safe, like we're not going to get caught.

I sort of like it too. Sure, it gets darker, but it's more than that. It's like shutting out all the crap I have to think about, all the stuff at home, at work, downstairs. Total freedom for another eleven minutes.

I edge forward, arms out, groping the air. She leans in for a kiss, but I dodge, act like it's too dark to find her lips and turn her around. I don't even know why I do it, just seems easier I guess.

I drop my trousers and step out of them. Now I'm in a shirt, boxers and socks. Horrible. Am I really going to have sex with my socks on? There's no time to get any more clothes off either of us. I steer her toward the king-size and then I hear an ugly crack. She yelps.

'Hear that? That was my shins smacking into the bed,' she grumbles.

'Sorry,' I mutter. 'You did ask for the curtains closed, right?'

She breathes in sharply, like she's going to say something, but nothing comes out. I don't know what she's pissed off about. Who's going to be looking at her legs anyway?

'I'll be more careful, I swear.'

Somehow I get her on all fours on the mattress. I can smell the cheap hotel soap on her body. Like those little pink slivers they give kids at school. I wonder if she washes here, or if she steals the soaps and uses them at home.

I lift up the skirt of her uniform and clamp my hands over her butt. It's a good arse, soft and an excellent shape, but even through her nylon pants her skin feels cold. This better not feel like having sex with a dead person, cause, I'm not sure I'm into that.

I know this time we're going to actually do it. Her hole is right there, underneath a single layer of fabric. I press my thumb where I think her slit is and the gusset of her knickers sticks to her. She pushes against my hand and makes a little moan.

Nine minutes.

Mandy reaches over to the bedside drawer and rattles it open. I can just make her out in the dark, fishing round for something inside. I move closer, not letting up. She finds a rubber and hands it to me.

She may be ready but I'm just not hard enough yet. It's the time, too much pressure. Like trying to fuck on the Crystal Maze. Got to come within three minutes or Richard O'Brien locks you in for the rest of the show. No one wants that. I had an uncle who was on the Crystal Maze, did quite well, but now's not the time to think about it.

Once I've got my dick out, I run my free hand up and down her thighs, a bit like I'm frisking her. I think about smacking her arse and decide it's not worth the risk. Her bare, rounded buttocks feel as smooth as -

I will not think about Richard O'Brien.

I try tugging on my nuts just a little to wake things up. Nothing. I close my eyes, and demand my brain think of something hot. Flashes of girls – ones I've fucked and ones I've seen through a PC screen reel through my head until they all blend into one. Skinny ones, fat ones, blondes on blondes as well as brunettes and redheads. Tight little college girls and wrinkly old grandmas. Black girls with massive tits and Asian chicks with their very own dicks. The images race faster. I try to rein them into focus, to turn that craving onto Mandy, sink myself into her. I screw my eyes up tight and my mind goes blank. Then out of the darkness -

Richard O'Brien. Richard O'Brien. Richard O'Brien.

LAUREN

The toilet stall is cramped and dirty. I can feel the heel of my shoes sticking to the grimy floor tiles. On the other side of the plastic door are at least a dozen women waiting for a cubicle. I can hear them, bitching to each other, clacking their heels and hastily puffing on fags. There's a lot of theatrics around sucking in smoke because it's banned in the club, a lot of giggling at their deviancy. While they're out there with their Marlboro Lights, I'm in here, trying for a bump of coke in peace.

Every now and then the door to the ladies opens, someone joins the queue for a cubicle, and the muffled beat of the DJ's latest track blasts out in utter clarity. Then it's back to the smoke and the bitching. I don't care if they form a line so long it snakes right out into the club, they can wait all night. I'm not going anywhere.

I cut a long, thin line of coke on the cistern using a credit card that was presented to me by my first London friend, a man with a large heart and an even larger wallet. The name on the card isn't mine, but it's the name I gave him and while it doesn't work anymore and he and I no longer talk, I like to think of it as a good luck charm on nights like this.

This place really is a shithole. I normally wouldn't even have sex in here, let alone do a line. The brightness of the powder makes the porcelain cistern look grey and I begin to think about the dirt and bacteria living on it. The thought is cut dead before it's had a chance to develop because without instructing it, my body bends down over the coke and chases the line clean away. I straighten up.

The rush is enough to drown any conscious thoughts for the next few seconds. There's nothing but me and the sound of my heart.

I flip open my compact and check my nose for residue. The woman in the mirror is barely recognisable, her twenty year old face framed with a blonde crop could

223

be anywhere between fourteen and forty, hidden under layers of thick, flawless make up. If it weren't for the seven inches of scar tearing down between her breasts, I'd question if this reflection even belonged to me.

Blood thumps through my ears from the coke hit, and I run my fingers over the scar, feeling my heart work overtime a few inches underneath it. Sounds drain away. I close my eyes, raise my head toward heaven and hold on to the feeling.

I'm rudely interrupted by a text on my phone.

> FROM: ASIANGUY
> YOUR SEAT IS GET
> TING COLD. NICO.

I snap the phone shut and shove it back in my purse. At least I've learnt a thing or two. First, Asian Guy is called Nico and second, if his name is Nico perhaps he's not Asian after all.

We've known each other all of a week and a half. He picked me up on The King's Road. I was trying to hail a cab when my heel snapped off in a cracked pavement. He offered me a lift home in his Lexus. It seemed rude to refuse.

This is the second time we've been out. The first was a members club in a private mews in Mayfair. This time it's a basement bar in Soho. I've only been in London nine months and I already know this kind of venue is not my scene. Half the crowd are underage and the other half seem like amateur sex offenders looking to turn pro. While Nico keeps feeding me free lines it is hard to complain to him.

The scar doesn't bother him either. Tonight I wore it on full display, cutting through my cleavage like a territorial marking and he didn't say a thing. But then, like most coke heads, Nico doesn't often look beyond the end of his own nose.

I unlock the cubicle door and a Spearmint Rhino reject tramps in before I am half way out. I sigh heavily, my sour Martini breath in line with her face as she pushes past.

I only understand her haste when another woman in the queue screeches. Cubicle door still open, the tramp is crouched unceremoniously over the bowl. Her top has ridden up, revealing a warped tattoo of Thumper, the rabbit from *Bambi*, stamped over her baby-fat. There's vomit everywhere: the tiles, the walls, her chest – and none in the toilet.

'Jesus,' she whimpers, clutching onto a string of plastic neon love beads around her neck.

'Jesus can't help you. He's dead.' I tell her and head back into the heat of the club.

It's too loud to talk in the club and I'm finding it hard to sit still next to Nico. I know what he wants. I'm supposed to sit here with my legs crossed, letting my dress ride up just a little while other men watch us enviously from the bar or the dance floor. My arm's twitching and the coke makes me want to run my mouth off.

He calls for a round of champagne and whispers something in my ear. I don't catch any of it; just feel a few pearls of spit against my neck. In the heat of the club it's almost cooling.

He thinks he's going to fuck me tonight. Including the ride home the day we met this is the third time we've gone out. Enough for a nice girl to protect her reputation, but also the end of a free ride for a gold digger. If I don't put out, he won't call again. He has treated me these last few dates. Coke from his personal stash, quality stuff, not to mention a ten or twenty to snort it with each time I head to the ladies for a powdering. He bought me a watch too. Ugly gold thing, but probably worth a hundred. He expected me to wear it tonight, so I left it at home. Whatever he's given me, it's all just a precursor, an opening negotiation for sex.

I pull out my purse, crack open a pill from its foil shell and drop it in my drink. It starts to dissolve immediately.

'What's wrong?' he asks.

'Nothing,' I tell him, 'Headache.'

'Too much coke.' he sneers and turns back to watch the crowd.

He's already downed his champagne and when he's making eyes at the waitress I swap his empty with my full glass. He drinks it without question.

The clock is ticking. I whisper in his ear, 'I think you're going to remember tonight for a long time.'

He will, just not for the reason he expects.

6252109R00138

Printed in Great Britain
by Amazon.co.uk, Ltd.,
Marston Gate.